RUPERT

Born in Brighton, musician and au

composer and sound designer for t.

has also released a number of solo albums on labels such as Third

Kind, Spun Out Of Control and Modern Aviation.

He lives in Switzerland with his wife and two children.

ALSO BY RUPERT LALLY:

Solid State Memories

Rupert Lally

BACKWATER

This paperback edition published 2022
Text ©2022 Rupert Lally

ISBN: 9798448995644
Imprint: Independently published

for
anthony charles lally
[1937 - 2014]

BACKWATER

chapters:

Part One: The Journey There:

Part Two: The Journey Back:

part one:

the journey there

Time is a river of passing events - a rushing torrent.

Greek Proverb

chapter one:
everything changes

ife watched the first pinky bronze rays of the sun break over the trees on the far hills to her left. She'd meant to get a few hours sleep after helping Betha and Nareena clean and prepare her father's body but, after lying on her bedding for a short while, she had gotten up again and walked down the hillside to the bottom of the waterfall and sat there watching as the sky turned slowly from black to deep blue until finally a small strip of pink had appeared between the trees.

Her father had died just as the sun was leaving the sky the day before. Soon its light would illuminate his body as it lay, wrapped in linen, in a skiff in the middle of the central chamber of the council broch. As was the custom, it would stay there throughout the day as members of the settlement came to pay their respects and bring offerings. Then, late in the afternoon, his body would be carried down the hillside to the stone circle near where she sat. Soon, those tasked with preparing the circle for the ceremony would arrive and begin work, but for now Aife was alone and she clung to her last few moments of precious solitude like the valuable commodity they were.

Everything would change from this point onwards.

As the daughter of one of the council, she had grown up in the broch, a multi-storied roundhouse, with the other council members and their families. Membership of the council could only be passed to a male descendant, however, and so Aife's father's place would be taken by her cousin, Cahal, who would move into the broch with whichever of the women he decided to marry and eventually house his family there; whilst Aife would have to lodge with whatever other relatives she had (in this case Cahal's parents) until she found a husband and could move in with him.

She didn't resent Cahal. Her cousin wasn't aggressive or impetuous and was certainly better suited to the business of helping to govern their settlement than most of the other young men here, who still seemed like little boys in overgrown bodies. More recently, as her father's health had declined, he'd seemed almost as unhappy about the reshuffling of their respective positions as she was.

She remembered one day, about a month before, when he'd asked her to go for a walk with him. They'd meandered aimlessly through the settlement, stopping to inspect the animals and generally making small talk, until they'd eventually ended up at almost this exact spot. Then the conversation had turned to her father's health and the day they both knew was coming.

"He seemed a little better, when I visited him the other day," Cahal had said, "clearer in his thoughts, perhaps..."

"He changes from day to day, but I'm sure your visit made him more lively than he might have been otherwise. Did you talk about council business?"

"A little. Bricriu is pushing for us to increase the trade of our crystal further than the outlying settlements."

"Wouldn't that mean a large increase in production, if we need to cope with the extra demand?".

"He and Malvyn believe that with our current surplus, the actual increase in work would be small enough to make little difference to the miners."

"What do the rest of the council say?"

"Henwas and your father are opposed. Neese wants more accurate information on what the demand might be, but is ultimately in favour, if it will mean a sharp increase in trade and prosperity for our settlement."

"What's your view?" she asked him.

"At the moment, I don't have one. Which is no doubt why your father wanted to confide in me and also to find out if Malvyn or Bricriu had approached me to side with them when the time comes."

"And have they?"

"Not yet, but I've no doubt one or the other will, eventually. I must say I can't see anything wrong in the increase in trade that further distribution might bring."

"Do we need it though? What will further trade bring us in the end? We have more than enough food and produce through our own means and trade with the outliers. I think he's right: further trade serves only to satisfy Malvyn and Bricriu's ambition for more power, rather than any clear benefit to the settlement."

"And what happens when we have another sudden cold spell, like that of the spring before last, when many of our root crops died before they could be harvested? The outliers wouldn't be able to help us because they would be facing the same problem, but trade with settlements further away might make all the difference in times such as that."

"Surely better methods of protecting the crops from the weather or preserving them longer from the previous season would solve that problem too? We live in harmony with the outliers, there has been no conflict with any settlement for generations, but what happens when it becomes widely known how much of our crystal can be mined here? How long before someone decides they want more than we are willing to give?"

"That's your father talking..."

"Maybe, but he has a point and that Malvyn and Bricriu won't acknowledge that danger seems reckless to him...and to me."

Cahal looked down at the ground. "I didn't ask for this, you know?"

"I know, and no one here knows better than I how difficult your task will be. My father always said the point of a council of five was not just so there would always need to be a majority, but also so that one member could make a difference. I don't think my father wants you to share his view unless you think it's the right one for you."

"But you think it's the right one."

"I do, but then what makes my opinion more worthy than that of another?"

"So, what would you do then…if you were in my position?"

"Gather more opinions. So far you only have four, or five if you count mine as well. Maybe you should ask others in the settlement? That way, when the time comes you can be sure you've made a decision which is truly right for the majority."

"Sometimes I wonder if the rules shouldn't be changed. You certainly sound more prepared for this than I am."

"You'll be fine." Aife replied and as she did, a small pang of sadness welled inside her because it was at that moment she realised that he actually would be.

Matthew sat in a chair, next to his father's bed. He could hear the lawyers and the doctor conferring in the hallway outside, despite the steady beep of his father's heart monitor and the fact that they tried to keep their voices down. It was clear what was being discussed, even if he couldn't make out every word.

His father was dying.

The lawyers were trying to ascertain from the doctor whether it was a question of hours or days.

Matthew looked over at his father, struggling for breath on the ventilator, his skin flushed pink. A shaft of sunlight lay across the bed and Matthew could see specs of dust floating around in the air above his father's head. Almost like a halo, he thought to himself.

He leaned over and took his father's hand in his own. There was no reaction. His condition had worsened yesterday evening and since then his father had remained unconscious. It was clearly only a matter of time before the decision was made to switch off the ventilator and let him slip away.

"Dad?" Matthew whispered into his father's ear, "if you can hear me... I want you to know, it's alright to let go. I'll be ok...I love you."

His father didn't respond, of course. Matthew patted his hand and placed it back on the bed.

Outside, the hushed voices finished their conversation and Matthew suspected a decision had been made.

Aife got up and walked back up the hillside past the waterfall. Normally, at this time of the day, there would be a steady stream of miners carrying carts back and forth from the mine underneath it, but today, as mark of respect for the death of one of the council, all work had ceased.

Whilst there were many local mines in the hills around them, digging natural ores out of huge pits, what Aife's settlement mined in the hollowed out caverns behind the waterfall was something quite different: a pinkish crystalline rock, highly prized for use as jewellery, enabling the settlement to trade freely and easily for copper and tin which the smiths forged into bronze for tools, weapons or foodstuffs.

She passed Anghus, Owyn, and Ferghus on her way back up the hill. They were part of the group tasked with preparing the ceremonial circle. They all stopped and Owyn and Ferghus offered their sympathies to her, whilst Anghus simply held her in his huge arms in silence for a moment before saying,

"He was one of the greatest men this settlement has ever known and the ancestors will welcome him with great joy, but I'm sure he would have given anything to have more time here with you."

Aife blushed at this and, for the first time since her father's death, tears came readily to her eyes. Such outspoken sentiment was not typical of Anghus. He was usually slightly taciturn, though never in a bad tempered way. She liked him a great deal, not only because he was married to one of her best friends, but also because he was the sort of person who was content to let their actions speak for themselves. Having grown up in the environment of the council, where every decision had to be ratified and great emphasis was placed on presenting an appearance of harmony, whether there was or not; somebody like Anghus was a refreshing change.

He must have noticed the tears, even as she blinked them away. "Idelisa was looking for you," he said, "she and others are already preparing the communal space for the feast tonight."

"Of course, I need to get on and help them with it. I'll go and find her now."

He put his hand on her shoulder and nodded before turning away and following Owyn and Ferghus down the hill. Aife walked on up to the settlement stopping briefly at the pig pens to look in on her favourite sow, Cinnia, who'd had a litter of piglets just a few days previously. Then, she crossed the wooden walkway over the river to where the large crannog-style community buildings stood on wooden stilts, looking out over the waterfall and the valley beyond.

She paused as she walked across the walkway. As a child, this had been her favorite spot in the entire settlement and she had spent many hours standing here, trying to see as much of the world beyond as she could. Looking down, you could follow the river until its course bent in the far distance and the tree-line covered its path. On a clear late summer morning, like today, you could catch shimmering glimpses of what must be the river through the trees further on.

"Can you see Backwater from there?" Her father had once asked her.

"Of course not!" the small version of her had replied, "that's much too far away."

Backwater was a local legend, passed down to each new generation, probably stemming from the very beginnings of a settlement here. The river, that thundered over the waterfall beneath the walkway on which she stood, began as a large spring somewhere in the mountains, high above. Common sense dictated that the river had to eventually flow into a larger body of water or back into the ground at some point. Backwater was the name given to the place where, supposedly, this took place. It was the place where the bodies of the dead went on their last journey, before being transmuted into their eternal forms.

"Is there really a Backwater?" she had asked her father that day.

"I don't see why not...but perhaps, as with most things in this world, it's not what we think it is..."

The answer had been typical of her father, always showing her that there were no true answers, only more questions. Maybe, as Cahal had half suggested, he had hoped the rules would change and she could be part of the council and, if so, needed to be prepared for that possibility.

He had certainly taken great pains to make sure she hadn't just learned the normal skills that the other girls in the settlement had to learn. In addition to cooking, sewing, pottery, animal husbandry and the application of herbs for healing, he had seen to it that she had also been taught swordsmanship, hunting, archery, and even basic metallurgy - which had been the most controversial of all, as women were no more allowed in the smelting chambers than on the council. However, he'd used his influence once again and Einion, the chief smith, had shown her the rudiments of how the copper and tin that they traded for could be harnessed and moulded into useful forms in a series of private lessons, when the chambers were empty.

Most of the adults in the settlement regarded it as an indulgence on the part of a doting father, left to bring up a child by himself. Some, like Malvyn, had actively quarrelled with her father about it, saying it wasn't preparing Aife for the life she was going to have. To this her father had simply replied that no one knew what their life was going to be and that it was far better to be prepared with skills that one might never use, than to trust that life would work out just the way you had planned. Privately, he had added that if Malvyn, whose two children Oriana and Eghan often made fun of Aife's additional lessons, took as much interest in his own offspring and the happiness of the settlement as he

10

seemed to in Aife's education, life here would be much better for it.

Eghan and Oriana weren't the only ones who made fun of her, though. Aife knew that many of the other children resented the fact that she was allowed to learn different things than the rest of them.

The joshing of the boys had ceased as soon as she had proved she could wield a sword or bow as good, if not better, than most of them. The few who had persisted, often led or encouraged by Eghan, had learnt to keep their counsel once Cahal and Anghus had made it clear that anyone who tried to pick on her would answer to them.

With the girls it wasn't so simple. Oriana's continual taunting was one thing, but her friend Ethne, who clearly wished that she had been born a boy, openly seethed resentment that Aife was allowed to break out of their gender-defined roles when she wasn't. Even her best friend, Idelisa, was often unsympathetic when Aife complained of how unhappy she was.

"There you are, I was getting worried..."

Aife turned and saw Idelisa standing by the entrance to the communal space. She walked over to where Aife was standing and embraced her.

"Anghus told me you were looking for me. I didn't mean to worry you," Aife said, "I couldn't sleep after helping Betha and your mother prepare him, so I went for a walk down by the river. I just needed some time alone."

"Nobody could begrudge you that, after all the time you spent looking after him at the end. I'm so sorry for your loss, I know how much he meant to you...and he knew how much you loved him, I've no doubt about that."

For the second time that morning, Aife fought back the tears but Idelisa saw them and held her once more. "It's alright, you can cry. No one expects you to pretend you're anything other than heartbroken."

"It's not as if I didn't know this day was coming," she replied, wiping away her tears, "you'd think I'd be better prepared..."

"There isn't a way to prepare for this," said Ethne. She came over to the pair of them and put her arms around Aife as well.

Ethne's father had died two springs ago, collapsing suddenly one morning whilst tending to the animals. Like Aife, she was an only child and her father's death had also brought a change in her circumstances. With no brothers or sisters to help, she was now responsible for looking after their family's animals. All talk of when she might find a husband had ceased, which suited Ethne just fine. It was, Aife had mused at the time, perhaps easier to decide for yourself what sort of life you wanted when you were the daughter of a farmer, rather than that of a council member.

In any event, it had ended any jealousy between her and Aife and whatever difficulties she might have had with Idelisa, were now also long forgotten. The three confided in each other constantly. They had been the first to know when Anghus proposed to Idelisa, though the union surprised no one in the settlement and they'd both been at Idelisa's side when she'd given birth to Bevyn, with Ethne remarking how much easier and quicker the process seemed to be with pigs than people. Both Ethne and Idelisa had also helped Aife with her father, when his health began to deteriorate, looking after him for a while so that Aife could have a break or do some chores. Sometimes Idelisa had brought little Bevyn along with her, which had pleased Aife's father no end. Bevyn was now almost two and big for his age, just like his father. He was a sweet boy, though and had loved listening to the stories Aife's father had told him.

The three of them broke apart and Aife followed Ethne and Idelisa into the communal space, where they and others had been laying out benches and tables. The whole settlement would to eat here tonight after the ceremony. In the far corner, where the space let out on a small sheltered courtyard, those tasked with cooking were already preparing the hearths and the huge bronze pots they would need. Aife could see the carcasses of several pigs and sheep hanging there, ready to be cut up for the stew that evening; whilst further away she could just make out Donaghy and Karney digging a pit for the midden. In another corner of the space some of the settlement's older children had been given the job of washing and preparing the vegetables for the stew, whilst others, under the supervision of Idelisa's mother

Nareena, were making dough for the many breads being baked. Bevyn was standing next to her and when he saw Aife he ran over to her and hugged her leg. She picked the boy up in her arms and carried him back to Nareena.

"Idelisa took him to see your father's body," Nareena said as took her grandson in her arms. "He's too young to understand really, but I think he realises that his friend is gone". The little boy turned his head away and buried it in his grandmother's shoulder, as if trying to blot out the loss.

"They were very fond of each other," Aife said, stroking Bevyn's hair, "my father loved it when Idelisa brought him to visit. Though he would never have admitted it to me, I think he would loved grandchildren of his own to play with."

"Perhaps, but from what I knew of your father, he wanted you to do what was best for you, not for him - that's all parents ever want for their children. You'll meet someone in time, I'm sure of it. Don't let thoughts of how things could have been different creep into your mind and spoil your memories of him. You were a good daughter to him and he loved you. That is all that matters."

Aife nodded and left Nareena to her work. She walked back to where Ethne and Idelisa were decorating one of the long tables with petals. At that moment, Oriana appeared and came over to where the three of them were standing.

"Deepest sorrow for your loss, Aife," Oriana said. "My father asked me to check if you needed any help in removing your things from the council broch. If so, I'd be happy to offer my assistance."

"You don't waste any time," said Ethne, with a smirk. "Of course you'll be happy to help, you'll be only too pleased to see the back of her..."

"It is unfortunate that on such a sad day, the business of the settlement and the council must continue," she replied, "but that is the way of things, I meant no disrespect."

"Of course you didn't," said Aife, drawing Oriana's attention back to her, whilst Ethne made rude gestures behind her back. "Please tell your father, I will see to it as soon as I'm done here. I have already moved most of my belongings to my Uncle's home, I'm sure I can manage the rest alone, but thank you for your kind offer."

"Very well," she replied and nodding to both Ethne and Idelisa, left them to their work.

"She never changes," said Idelisa, once Oriana was out of earshot.

"Aye, she's a piece of work that one," said Ethne. "I hear she has designs on your cousin, Aife..."

"Cahal? I can't see he'd have much interest in her."

"Perhaps, but he has to marry someone, Aife," Idelisa replied, "and I know he and Anghus have talked about it."

"What? Am the only one in the entire settlement who knew nothing about this?"

"I don't think Cahal has decided anything...but even you must see why many would wish to see it happen."

"I can see why Oriana would wish for it to happen. It would guarantee her place in the broch and strengthen her father's, and eventually her brother's, position on the council. How could Cahal ever vote against them if he's married to their daughter and sister?"

"She's certainly not stupid, I'll give her that," said Ethne. "If things go to plan she'll end being the power behind the whole council. Can you imagine how insufferable she'll be then?"

"I can't believe Cahal would even consider it."

"Your cousin's clever," said Ethne, "but he's still just a man. What chance has he if Oriana, her father, and your uncle want him to marry her?"

(5)

They removed Matthew's father from the ventilator and mercifully he didn't hold on for long afterwards. There were words of condolence from the doctor and the small team of nurses, before Matthew and the lawyers left them to make the arrangements for the body whilst they reconvened in the kitchen, with talk turning to business and Matthew's inheritance of the family estate almost immediately.

There would be some small settlement for Matthew's mother - despite the fact that neither he nor his father had seen her in over 10 years - mostly in order to make sure she didn't make any further claims on the estate. Otherwise, the bulk of the money and his father's property would go to Matthew. He had no brothers or sisters and his father was also an only child. Matthew's grandparents were both long dead, so that left only him: A 15 year old, worth a small fortune, with an army of lawyers and business managers to watch over him or perhaps, more simply, that he would need to watch over - he was sure most still saw him as the small child he had once been. They probably hoped he'd be content to go back to school and leave the running of his father's finances to them.

If so, they were wrong.

Matthew had no intention of heading back to school yet. It was almost the end of term anyhow. Combined with the upcoming holidays that gave him almost a month before he needed to come to any firm decision about his future. He wanted to consider his options properly, as well as get to grips with all his father's assets. The lawyers and business managers were reassured that he would not do anything drastic and that he would speak to them all in good time.

Yes, he thought, *that's what I need - time.*

Once she was done, Aife went to the council broch and collected the few things she had left there, packed them into a small handcart and wheeled it back across the wooden walkway to her uncle Tanguy's home.

Her uncle was busy working on the food for the feast so only his wife, Fianna, who had spent the morning collecting flowers and herbs to decorate the communal space, was home when Aife got there. The two of them spent some time talking about Aife's father and then, just as Aife was about to leave, Cahal arrived.

"Hello Aife," he said, after he had kissed his mother on the cheek. "I didn't expect to see you here, I thought you'd still be busy with the preparations for the feast tonight or having a rest, I don't suppose you got much sleep last night..."

"No," Aife replied, "but I'll have a rest later on before the ceremony starts. I brought the last of my things over from the broch, on the handcart, so if you want to use it to carry some of your stuff over there, we can do."

"That sounds like a good idea, Cahal," said his mother. "I've already bundled up some of your things, you can take them with you when you go and save Aife having to push the cart back on her own."

Cahal collected the belongings his mother had packed for him and he and Aife walked back to the broch with them. Once they were out of her aunt's earshot, Aife seized the chance to ask Cahal about the possibility of him marrying Oriana.

"I was going to talk to you about it," he admitted, slightly sheepishly, "there just never seemed to be the right moment with everything that was going on with your father..."

"But is it really what you want? You never used to like her or Eghan."

"She's not the same as she was when we were children. Whenever we've talked together alone, I've seen a different side to her. She's not the arrogant, insensitive monster you make her out to be. She doesn't really go around acting like she's better than everyone else..."

"She still seems to do it whenever I'm around..."

Cahal sighed. "It's certainly no secret that the two of you have never got along, but maybe some of that is also your doing..."

"My doing? Surely you're not serious, Cahal? Oriana has never been anything other than horrible to me!"

"But don't you see? A lot of that was just jealousy because you were allowed to do the things she wasn't; the two of you are more alike than you realise."

"The only thing that Oriana and I have in common is that, as daughters of council members, we both lose our places in the council broch when our fathers die. Unlike her, that prospect doesn't fill me with such terror that I'm prepared to marry anyone just to keep my position there."

"Is that really what you think? That the only reason she could possibly have for wanting to marry me is to keep her position?"

"You don't think her timing is a little suspect?"

"I think the fact that you think it is, says more about your view of her than her actual intentions. Tell me this isn't just about you not being allowed to take your father's seat on the council?"

"Surely you know me better than that, Cahal?"

"I thought I did, now suddenly I'm not so sure. I'd always wondered if, secretly, you didn't resent me for being the one who would take your father's place on the council. So often you act as if you're my teacher...tell me, what do you believe is going to happen, now that I'm on the council? Did you think you were going advise me all the time? That I would come and talk to you about everything that goes on there, just as my uncle did? That's not going to happen, Aife."

Cahal's words stung, there was no use in denying it. Whilst Aife had never wanted to control or influence Cahal's decisions once he became part of the council, she had hoped that he might occasionally confide in her - after all, she did know the workings of the council every bit as well as he did. She could feel the hot beginnings of tears forming again, but she fought them back and this time her eyes did not betray her.

"Are you going to make this same speech to Oriana? If so, you should do it now so you can discover how true her affections really are. That would certainly be better than waiting and being disappointed after you're married, when she takes her father's side on a matter that you and he disagree on!"

"Do you really think so little of me, that you believe that I would let my decisions for the council be compromised by the person I chose to marry?"

"No, I think a great deal of you, Cahal, but this is an impossible position you're putting yourself in! This isn't something that will go away when Malvyn dies, either. Eghan is just as eager and ambitious as his father and even more impetuous. In binding yourself to this family through marriage, you make it incredibly difficult for you to ever stand against them on council matters and by doing that, risk making a mockery of everything the council is supposed to stand for!"

"You don't think I've considered this?" Cahal's temper was being to rise.

"Clearly not enough, if you're still thinking about marrying her!" Aife replied and instantly wished she hadn't.

"I'm sorry you feel that way," he said stiffly. "I'd hoped whatever animosity still lay between you and Oriana might have been put aside out of respect for my happiness, but I see now that can't happen." He pushed the handcart forward and left Aife standing there.

chapter two:
swords & ceremonies

I t was mid afternoon. Having been placated by the news that Matthew would have further discussions about his future after his father's funeral, the lawyers and business managers had left him alone to grieve in private. He found it difficult to do so, however. The nature of having to concentrate on the business side of death had left him momentarily numb. Instead, he wandered rather aimlessly around his late father's study, occasionally touching some object or another that had meant something to his dad, and reading the obituaries and tributes paid to his father in the news or social media.

His father had worn the mantle of wealth lightly, more than content to let the team of accountants and lawyers take care of the family's wealth or investments, leaving him free to concentrate on his true passion.

Many of his mementos surrounded Matthew now in their various display cases. Some, undoubtably, would be bequeathed to various museums, but for the time being they remained where they had stood for the last

23

twenty five years or more. Anything from before the Romans destroyed whatever native cultural heritage we had and replaced it with their own, was how his father had once described his varied collection. There were sundry arrow heads and pieces of pottery, as well as a few bits of jewellery and numerous swords in various states of completeness.

At that moment, one particular cabinet caught Matthew's eye. Its contents he knew only too well: a medium sized crystalline rock, a sword and a few small pieces of jewellery which had all been found as part of the same dig, shortly before he'd been born.

The pinkish coloured crystal was lepidolite. Its discovery amongst the dig had caused both excitement and some serious debate amongst various scholars. Firstly, because there were no known lepidolite deposits in the surrounding area of the excavation site and secondly, because it was not known what use people of that time would have had for it. Many had claimed that it might have been from a later time and should be ignored as a find from this particular period. However, Matthew's father had never wavered in his assertion that the lepidolite was clearly from the same era as the rest of the finds.

The controversy over the lepidolite had rather overshadowed the rest of what had been found but ultimately, it was the sword that had most fascinated Matthew's father. He vividly remembered the day his father had put it in his hands as a small child.

"Notice anything unusual?" he had asked Matthew.

Matthew had studied the sword intently, there was a slightly faded emblem of a spiral, near the hilt, like one third of the triskelion symbol found on so many European Neolithic and Bronze Age artefacts, but otherwise it seemed unremarkable.

"Now feel this one," his father had said, handing Matthew a similar sword. Matthew now held a sword in each hand.

"This one's slightly lighter," he said, holding up the sword found with the lepidolite.

"That's right, that's because that sword is not made of bronze."

"But it looks like bronze."

"I know, but it isn't."

"Then what metal is it?" Matthew had asked.

"That's the problem - I don't really know."

[2]

If Aife had been entertaining any second thoughts about what she planned to do, they dissipated completely after her talk with Cahal.

She returned to the council broch hoping, correctly as it turned out, that most of its inhabitants would now be busy either preparing for tonights festivities or their daily tasks, leaving the central chamber where her father's body lay, deserted. She slipped in quietly and edged along the side of the inner wall, keeping to the shadows until she was sure there was no-one about.

Her father's body lay in a skiff, on a small plinth in the centre of the chamber. She could see that many members of settlement had already brought offerings and left them around the base of the plinth: pieces of metalwork or jewellery, some beautiful pieces of polished jade and flint, several swords which had cracked during the forging process - making them useless as weapons but still highly prized as gifts - as well as shards from beautifully decorated pots. .

Aife's father's sword had been placed in the skiff by Aife herself, when she had prepared his body with Betha and Nareena. She had debated with herself long and hard about the sword. Traditionally, great warriors or leaders such as her father were buried with their weapons, just as skilled tradesmen were buried with a set of their tools. There were no shortage of swords in the settlement. Aife had been given her own by her father when she had finished her education and she had it with her now, strapped to her back, beneath her clothes. She'd brought it with her specifically for the purpose of exchanging it with her father's. Whilst she doubted anyone would begrudge her taking it, it would probably be frowned upon; which is why she wanted to make the exchange while no-one else was around.

At first glance, the two swords looked extremely similar, even down to the distinctive spiral emblem on its hilt, which was why Aife was confident no-one would notice the switch, even when they were packing the rest of the offerings into the skiff. Her father had deliberately commissioned Einion, the blacksmith, to make Aife an identical sword to his own and that was how she had discovered the truth about her father's weapon: when Einion confided to her how hard it had been to create a similar piece. Einion had struggled (an admission that did not come easy to the blacksmith) because he hadn't made Aife's father's sword and was convinced no that local smith, either here or in any of the outlying settlements could have done so either.

It was made from a metal that he'd never seen before.

The swords and tools alloyed from the two metals from local mines were good and strong. Far more so than weapons or tools made from just melting either of the components by themselves or those made from flint, as had been done previously. They were tools that would last a lifetime and more, if looked after. As good as they were, however, they would become dull through regular use and need re-sharpening after a time. Her father's sword never did. Thinking back, even to when she had been a small child, she had never seen her father do anything to maintain it, other than wipe it down with a piece of old cloth. Despite this, it remained as razor sharp as if it had been newly made the day before.

Many had admired the sword over the years but her father had always deflected such comments, saying something like: "What this old thing? It looks much grander than it really is. It's not much use for anything these days, but I keep it for sentimental reasons..."

When pressed for the story of how he came by it, he would usually mumble something vague about winning it in a game of chance or finding it in a forest beyond the outlying settlements when he'd travelled as a young man. The only consistent element to all these stories was their inconsistency - he never told the same tale about the sword's origin twice.

Just then she heard footsteps and voices and pressed herself back against the wall hoping that the shadows around the edges would be enough to hide her presence. She soon recognised the pair of voices once they got a bit nearer: Malvyn and Bricriu, deep in discussion.

"...of course, I understand the delicacy of the situation, but I'm not asking for a definite decision, merely the council's permission to make an initial foray to explore our options..." Bricriu was saying, as the pair entered the chamber.

"My dear Bricriu..." Malvyn replied, in his usual smooth manner, "...I understand completely and if the decision were only mine to give, then you should have it immediately. However, even you must understand that some patience and diplomacy is required in this matter. With Llyr's death, I have little doubt that much of the opposition to our proposal will dissipate, but it would be tactless to suggest even such an initial foray, with his passing still so fresh in the minds of the rest of the council and the settlement."

"If we are to begin any form of trade agreement, we must have it settled before the first frost comes. Mid-summer has already passed, the days are already beginning to shorten. Can we really afford to wait for the council and this settlement to finish mourning before we put this issue to a vote?"

"Of course not, and that's exactly my point: we can't wait that long, but if we try to force a vote on the issue now it will be counterproductive. I suggest that you begin your initial forays to see what potential trade options we have beyond the outlying settlements now, without consulting the council."

"That's highly irregular and would certainly reflect badly on both of us, should the council come to hear of it..."

"They won't and besides we're not talking about you entering into any agreements - you are to make no promises to any party, do you understand? This is simply to gather information about possible options. When the time comes to make a decision, the council will be glad to have accurate information about potential trade options and if anyone does question how you came by this intelligence, then we can say you learnt about it through your visits to the outliers. We'll give you a reason to visit some of the farther settlements in the next few days, inspecting one of the mines or the harvests or something like that. You won't be able to be away too long, a day or two at the most each time, so you'll have to make multiple forays, but gradually you can begin to seek out some potential traders. We can settle the details in a day or so. Now, if you wouldn't mind leaving me, I wish to pay my respects to our old friend, here..."

"Of course," Bricriu murmured.

Malvyn knelt down beside the plinth where the body lay. Aife kept completely still, worried that the slightest movement might give her away.

"I will miss you old friend, truly I will..." Malvyn said quietly to the corpse, "but, perhaps it is better that you are no longer here. The settlement needs to move forward and outwards, something you would have never have agreed to - even though you'd travelled widely yourself. I could never understand your reticence towards letting others know what we've accomplished here..."

Malvyn's words caused Aife think hard. Had she simply not noticed that her father wanted little to do with the outside world? Whilst he'd often talked about how he'd travelled a great deal as a young man, she had no recollection of her father ever venturing far from the settlement during her lifetime. With her mother dead, she had assumed that this was to do with him not wanting to leave her in the care of her uncle whilst he went away on council business, but perhaps there really had been something more to it than that. She remembered how vehemently he'd argued against trade beyond the outlying settlements:

"No good will come of it, Aife, mark my words," he had said. "What we have here is special. The abundance of our crystal under the waterfall is something others wish they had and whilst we must not covet it so that others grow jealous, we must also not be so free with it as to encourage them to think it should not belong to us."

Other memories came to her as she thought of this: Her father's delirium in his last days, when he'd say things that wouldn't make any sense. Aife tried to push the thoughts out of her mind. Like most children, Aife's father had always seemed 'old' to her, but it wasn't until these last few months, after a succession of fevers and illnesses had made him progressively weaker, that she had begun to accept that he was no longer the man he'd been previously. Her father as whatever shell remained, she could accept; just as she could the memory of the strong, sometimes stern, but always kind man who had raised her. The memory of him as a frail, frightened, ageing baby however, was something she wished she could forget as quickly as possible.

When Malvyn eventually stood up and left the chamber, Aife seized her chance and hurriedly exchanged the swords. Then she walked back over the bridge to her uncle's home, hoping that no-one would stop her to offer their condolences on the way.

Fortunately, no one did. Her aunt had obviously gone out to run some errands, so she was free to remove her father's sword and stow it under her bedding, without worrying about any prying eyes. She lay down, meaning only to rest for a short while, but instead fell quickly into a deep sleep.

[3]

Sleep came to Matthew too, eventually. Despite feeling tired and drained for most of the day, he had been worried that, having so much on his mind, he wouldn't be able to sleep when the time came. However, a nice meal cooked by Mrs Gilbert and a couple of glasses of a single malt that he found in his father's drinks cabinet had helped considerably.

Despite his ease at drifting off, his sleep was filled with uneasy dreams of his father, often taking place in his study or at the site of an archeological dig. In each case, his father asked for his help in looking for something, but was always vague as to what the object was. Several times he thought he might have found the desired object, only for his father to shake his head sadly or become irritable and tell Matthew he wasn't looking properly.

After one particularly frustrating episode, where his father seemed to be constantly getting farther and farther away from him every time he broke off his search, Matthew found himself awake in his room once more. As his eyes adjusted to the gloom he realised there was someone in the room with him.

"Who's there?" he called out, but the figure didn't answer. The man moved out of the shadows a little. He held the sword made of the strange metal in his outstretched hands, as if offering it to Matthew. His hair was white and his face was marked by a large scar that extended from just above his left eye, down the side of his cheek and almost touched the edge of his mouth.

Matthew reached for the sword and, at that moment, woke up properly this time. He was no longer in bed but sitting at the desk in the corner of his room. Had he gotten up in the night, gone to the desk and then fallen asleep again? He had no memory of it, if so. All he could remember now was the dream, the details of which were now already fading from his mind. He remembered they had been about his father and another man with a scarred face.

He looked down at the desk in front of him and saw that he'd written some numbers on a piece of paper there. As he studied them more closely, he realised what they must be from the way they were grouped together.

They were G.P.S. co-ordinates.

[4]

The next thing Aife was aware of was her aunt gently shaking her awake.

"Wake up, Aife," she was saying, "the sun's already low in the sky and you need to get ready. There's some fresh water in the basin for you to wash with..."

Aife sat up groggily, found the small earthenware basin that her aunt had placed beside her and splashed some water over her face. She then picked up the basin and carried over to a small table in the corner where she slept, which to spare any awkwardness now she was living there had been divided from her aunt and uncle's sleeping quarters by a curtain-like piece of animal hide. This was unusual. In Aife's time people's houses were, essentially, one large chamber, centred around a hearth in the middle. Families slept together, in a single room. Either because she was worried that, coming from the broch, Aife might not be used to this or perhaps simply that she didn't like the idea of her husband being able to see her fifteen year - old niece's naked body, Fianna had suggested the piece of animal hide. Aife felt sure that both hoped her stay with them would be temporary and that she'd soon find herself a husband and move in with him. Behind the hide, she undressed fully, laying her day gown, tunic and long woollen skirt on a small stool and began to wash herself all over. When she was done she put on her ceremonial gown and braided her hair.

Along with her aunt and uncle, she walked across the bridge to the broch, where the council members stood waiting alongside the body in the central chamber. At the signal from Malvyn, the four other members, Henwas, Neese, Bricriu and Cahal, lifted the skiff on to their shoulders, using a framework of wooden poles for support and began to proceed out of the broch with Malvyn out in front of them, carrying a lighted torch.

Aife, Fianna and Tanguy walked behind them as the group carrying the skiff made its way slowly down the hillside to the base of the waterfall. The other members of the settlement, some holding torches, lined the way down. As they passed by, they too fell in behind Aife and the others so that the procession grew to include everyone from the settlement. Once at the circle, Anghus and the others took charge of the body from the council and gently lowered it into the water, with some actually standing in the river holding on to the skiff so that it wouldn't float away until the desired moment. Malvyn used his torch to ignite the ceremonial fire at the centre of the circle and then, as the sun began to dip below the trees on the other side of the valley, began his speech.

"Members of our beloved settlement, we are gathered here to pay witness to our friend and council member, Llyr, as he begins his final journey towards the realm of the ancestors. Though he with be sorely missed, not least by his daughter, Aife, and his brother, Tanguy, he will be forever remembered as one of this settlement's most important figures: never stinting in his belief in the importance of the life we have built here. Knowing that, as the eldest son, he would one day assume the mantle of council member from his father; he sought to widen his knowledge of our land as much as he could when he was younger, travelling far and wide as an emissary. It was through his work that many of our trade ties with the outlying settlements came to pass and he was one of the most fervent champions of our current role in working with the outliers to ensure that none of our settlements ever face severe hardship or starvation again. I want to assure each of you now, that this council will see to it that his scheme of mutual co-existence will only continue to grow and strengthen in the years to come - that, it seems to me, is the very least this community can do in tribute to his legacy.

However, he wasn't just an example when it came to the running of this settlement, he also showed great courage and determination on a personal level. After the loss of his great love, Deva, during the birth of their only child, most would have either stepped down from the council or entrusted the raising of their child to a relative, but he did neither. Instead, he managed to maintain the delicate balance of being both a committed leader of this community, as well as a devoted father to his child. Sadly, in this last year, his health began to fail and despite the care and attention of both his daughter and others here, he has now left us. Thus, we commit what is left of him to the river, that it will eventually reach Backwater where it will be transmuted into its eternal form and he will, once more, be re-united with Deva and live forever amongst the ancestors."

As he finished his speech, Malvyn nodded to Anghus and Ferghus, who let go of the skiff and the entire community watched as the current from the waterfall, pushed the body away to begin its journey downriver. Whilst the current was not that strong, the fading light meant that very soon the skiff was no longer visible. Once it could no longer be seen, the crowd gradually dispersed, moving slowly back up the hill and over the walkway to where the feast was waiting.

By the time Aife reached the community buildings the feast was already in full swing. She and her Aunt and Uncle were sat on the topmost table as guests of honour, along with Cahal and the rest of the council. Cahal barely made eye contact with Aife throughout the meal. She didn't have much time to notice, though, as the other members of the council, particularly Henwas who'd always gotten on well with her father, spent the entire meal regaling her and the rest of the table with stories of her father's exploits. It was all stuff she'd heard many times before, though she did not object as it pleased her to hear her father so warmly remembered. Equally, she wondered how much of this apparent fondness was really sincere and her mind wandered back to what she'd overheard in the broch that afternoon.

To anyone observing, however, she seemed the perfect embodiment of a loving daughter, dealing gracefully with the death of her father. Some even remarked on her good appetite "in the midst of grief", not noticing that for every piece of meat or bread she helped herself to, half would be surreptitiously stowed away in a piece of cloth under the table.

When the meal was over and the benches and tables at the centre of the space were removed and there was the customary music and dancing, Aife joined in enthusiastically at the beginning. She danced with her Uncle, Anghus, Cahal (who continued to avoid making eye contact with her and spent much of their dance looking in the direction of Oriana, who seemed to be doing the same), Henwas and even Malvyn, who used it as an opportunity to lean in far closer to than she would have liked and assure her that she could always come to him for advice or guidance in the future.

When she noticed Anghus standing in one corner of the community space by himself, she seized her opportunity and grabbed him by the elbow.

"Come on Anghus, you need some air, let's go outside for a moment..."

Anghus accompanied her outside without any objection. Away from the noise of the festivities her tone became more serious.

"I need your help, Anghus."

"Of course," he replied, blinking rapidly, "what do you need me to do?"

"I need you to talk to Cahal for me, he'll listen to you."

"Why wouldn't he listen to you?"

"We had an argument this afternoon about him marrying Oriana."

"He'll come 'round in a few days - just give him some time. I'm sure you didn't say anything he hadn't thought himself and anyway, maybe he needed to hear it from someone..."

"It's not about that. Malvyn and Bricriu are planning to begin trade negotiations without the rest of the council knowing. Bricriu will leave in a few days, supposedly to inspect the harvests or something like that, but in reality he's going to begin to find out if settlements beyond the outliers would want to trade with us. Cahal and the rest of the council need to know about this."

"How do you know all this?"

"I overheard Malvyn and Bricriu when I was in the broch this afternoon. They didn't know I was there..."

"You have to tell him this, Aife, it shouldn't be me. I'll come with you, we can talk to him together and if he refuses to listen to you, I'll make him listen, but this must come from you. He's bound to have questions, after all..."

"If I could, I would... just promise me you'll tell him. You'll understand why in a day or so."

"What are you going to do?"

"Promise me."

"Aye, I promise," he said, though she could tell he was worried, "just don't do anything stupid."

"Dear, Anghus...as if..." she kissed him on the cheek and gave him a hug.

"Are coming you back inside?"

"In a moment. You go on back though, before Idelisa wonders what I've done with you."

She watched him head back inside and then slipped quietly away. Most didn't even notice her departure until much later. Those that did simply assumed she was exhausted after such an emotional day and her aunt and uncle accepted that she had returned to their home to sleep. When they returned home much later, having both consumed a fair amount of food and drink themselves, they went straight to sleep without noticing anything out of the ordinary.

It would not be until late the following morning that Fianna actually noticed her absence. At first, she simply assumed that Aife had begun her chores early. It wasn't until midday, when she didn't return home to eat that she became worried. Drawing aside the animal hide curtain, she saw that Aife and her belongings were gone, . She immediately rushed over to the broch to find Cahal and ask him if he'd seen Aife that morning. Needless to say, he hadn't. He began searching the settlement. When he asked Anghus if he'd seen Aife, the big man looked worried and the two set off at once to check the skiffs moored by the river.

One was missing.

[5]

The funeral for Matthew's father was a week later. It was a cold and wet day, which kept the number of intrusive journalists to a minimum. The service was a quiet, secular affair at the local crematorium, with a few of his father's friends coming to pay their respects, so that it wasn't just Matthew and the lawyers at the service. Some of those present then came back to the house for drinks and sandwiches that the housekeeper had laid on. Matthew chatted amiably enough with those who came to offer their condolences, but in reality his mind was elsewhere.

For the last week all he had been able to think about was the dream and those co-ordinates he'd found written down afterwards.

He'd looked up the G.P.S. co-ordinates immediately and discovered they belonged to the siteof the dig where his father had discovered the sword and lepidolite all those years earlier. The land where the dig had taken place had belonged to his grandfather and was still owned by the family.

There was one problem, however.

The site had been excavated when a luxury apartment block had been proposed there. Once the site had been cleared of any historical finds, the apartments had been built, with Matthew's father retaining the penthouse suite as part of the deal. Matthew wondered if it might be possible for him to arrange a visit on the pretext of inspecting all of his families properties, now that he was the one who owned them.

Matthew took advantage of the occasion to drop the idea of visiting the apartment block into the conversation with one of his father's business managers, when he came over to offer his condolences once more. The manager, a man of about his father's age called Weston, thought Matthew's idea of visiting some of the properties he now owned an excellent idea and readily agreed to set up an appointment with the letting agent for Matthew to view the property within the next few days.

When the last of the mourners had gone, Matthew was left alone once more to think about that strange dream and its meaning. In the dream, the man with the scarred face had held out the sword to him; so clearly, in some subconscious way, it was significant. Matthew had no idea how, though.

He went to the glass display case and removed it from its stand. The metal felt strange under his fingers and he remembered that it had also given him a strange tingle when he had held it as a small boy. He put it into his rucksack, along with a torch and the building plan of the block of flats he'd manage to download from the internet a few days before.

Somehow, he felt it was important to have the sword with him when he visited the apartment block

chapter three:
journeys begin

[1]

By the time Cahal and Anghus realised she was missing, Aife had been floating downriver for about 12 hours.

She'd been planning on leaving for almost a month. Again and again during her father's illness she found herself sitting by the river's edge, thinking about following its current towards Backwater or whatever else might lie further downstream. Perhaps there would be nothing at all at the end of the river and she would just find a nice place to settle and live her life alone - that would also suit her just fine. She'd had enough of other people for a while and it certainly seemed preferable to spending her life being sneered at by the likes of Oriana. Perhaps, she might even return, after many years, when no-one cared anymore about who she was and what she did.

During one of these moments of fantasy, it had suddenly struck her that there was no reason why she shouldn't leave. She would miss Idelisa and Ethne, of course, but she knew that her love for them wasn't enough to keep her there. She also knew that if she told any of them of her plan they would try and stop her. Despite this, she had almost confided in Ethne several times but each time she'd thought better of it and kept quiet.

The thought of escape had kept her going during the most trying moments of her father's final weeks. She discovered to her horror that, in one sense, she was almost looking forward to the day her father would die. This had made her feel incredibly guilty and on several occasions she'd almost managed to convince herself not to leave after all.

After she'd left the feast, she'd returned briefly to her aunt and uncle's home and collected the last of her things: her other set of clothes and her father's sword; before walking down the slope, past the waterfall, to where she'd stashed her provisions, taking a skiff and paddling quietly away from the bank until the current began to take hold.

Away from the spill of the waterfall the current wasn't very strong, but it was constant and she hardly needed to use the paddle afterwards, except to make adjustments in her steering and avoid the occasional large boulder in the shallower parts. Around the middle of the following day, as the sun rose higher in the sky she began to feel tired. After feeling herself start to nod off at least once, she decided it would be safer to paddle the skiff over to one of the banks on either side and rest for a while.

She chose the right hand bank, mostly because she was slightly nearer to it, but also because its tree line extended closer to the river, so she could pull the skiff up onto the bank and hide both it and herself from view more easily. The relative lightness of the carved wooden skiff meant she was able to easily pull it ashore. Stowing it under a pair of trees, she climbed into it once more, and lay down. Despite the daylight and noise of birds in the trees around her, she was asleep almost as soon as she closed her eyes.

It was getting close to dusk when she awoke. She felt hungry and ate some of the food she had saved from the feast, which she had packed into a small leather pouch tied around her waist. She ate sparingly though, as she knew that once her cache of food was finished she would be forced to either hunt, fish or forage for her next meal as best she could. Once she was done, she found a secluded spot and defecated, before washing herself quickly in the river and refilled her pigs bladder full of drinking water. Then she dragged the skiff back to the river.

As she drifted along, she watched the last vestiges of daylight slip behind the hills and the stars begin to appear. She'd been fortunate so far in having a full moon to light her way in the dark. She could see it was beginning to wane however, which would mean she would no longer be able to travel at night. Traveling by day, whilst making it easier to spot any obstacles or bends in the river, brought its own problems. There were sure to be some settlements by the edge of the river and a young woman from another settlement, alone in a skiff, was bound to raise questions and unwanted attention.

She been continuing downriver at the same steady pace for what seemed like an hour when she noticed the current becoming stronger. She listened carefully. She couldn't hear any roar of water that would normally herald an approaching waterfall, just a more constant burbling. Perhaps there was a sharp bend up ahead. She strained her eyes to see ahead but either the moon had gone behind a cloud or the trees overhung so low in front of her that she could make little out. Suddenly the skiff rode up hard against an obstacle. Aife struck out with her paddle. She felt the end hit something solid and the sound of wood splintering. For a moment the skiff seemed to hang in the air, then it turned on its axis and flipped itself over. Aife felt herself falling for a few seconds before she went under the water.

Spluttering and gasping, she let go of the paddle and clawed her way to the surface, pulled down by her woollen clothes and the weight of her father's sword. Despite the darkness, she could just about make out the overturned skiff in front of her. She swam quickly towards it and managed to grab ahold of it, but with the increased weight from her wet clothes and the sword, the overturned skiff filled with water and slipped out from underneath her, making her go under again. When she came up for the second time, she could neither see nor feel the skiff anywhere near her. Treading water blindly, she tried not to panic and swam as hard she could to one side, knowing she must reach the river bank eventually. Her arms and legs began to feel heavier and she began to cough as she swallowed more and more water. Just then, her flailing arms caught the edge of a rock. She grasped it with both hands and with her last remaining ounce of strength, pulled herself up out of the water.

She lay there, coughing up water and laughing, saying to herself: "Almost father, almost..." before she eventually blacked out.

[2]

Matthew's visit to the apartment block was arranged for the week after his father's funeral. The letting agency had sent along one of their staff, an attractive young woman only a few years older than Matthew himself, to show him around the property and answer any questions he might have. Perhaps, unsurprisingly, Matthew found it it little difficult to concentrate during the tour and found himself nodding a great deal at whatever the agent told him. Even more unfortunate was that she didn't let him out of her sight during the tour, so he had no opportunity to explore the building on his own. After saying goodbye to her outside afterwards and promising to get in touch if he had any further questions (or even if he hadn't - she had added, writing down her phone number on the back of the agency's business card) Matthew walked halfway around the block and then waited, watching for the woman to get into her car and drive off. Once she was gone, he went back and hung around near the entrance for someone to leave, so that he could get into the building once more.

Once inside he headed for the basement, which he'd been shown briefly on the tour as it led through to the parking garage. Something told him he needed to get as close to the site of the archeological dig as possible. Next to the lift there were several storage and utility rooms which he'd spotted earlier. Judging from the architectural plans he'd downloaded in comparison with the photos from the dig, he guessed that the site of the dig must have been more or less where the larger of the two storage rooms was. He tried the door and, to his immense relief, found it wasn't locked.

(3)

It was impossible for Aife to judge how much time had actually passed by the time she came to again, but the sky was beginning to get light and now she could actually see what had happened. She was on the left hand bank of the river, after a sharp bend. A large tree had fallen three quarters of the way across the water, just after the bend - narrowing the current which had, in turn, eroded away the river bed beneath the tree creating a mini waterfall about five or six feet high. Due the summer heat the river level had dropped slightly, leaving the tree higher above the surface of the water, which is why her skiff had got stuck. Her father's burial skiff, weighted down as it was with tokens and gifts would have either just ridden over the tree trunk into the fall below or bobbed along it until the current carried it to the gap between it and the bank on the far side. She ruefully admitted to herself that if she'd been travelling in daylight she could have either avoided getting stuck against the tree or rowed to the bank on which she now stood and carried the skiff on land around the obstacle. There was no sign of her skiff now. She would have to continue on foot and she had lost all of her possessions, save the sword and the remaining food in the pouch around her waist, which she now ate quickly to keep her strength up.

She felt cold from her wet clothes and bruised from lying on the rocks. She set to work gathering wood for a fire and bashed two dry stones together to create the spark to light it. She used her father's sword to fashion a spear from a branch of a hazelnut bush and then used it to catch several fish, whilst standing in the shallow water by the edge of the bank. She cooked the fish over the fire, eating some and packing the rest up in a large leaf and storing in the pouch. By mid-morning, having dried her clothes by the fire, she felt sufficiently rested to continue her journey.

The undergrowth was thick and the going was slow. At times she needed to hack her way through using the sword. She continued to follow the path of the river as much as possible, but at times the bank was so steep that she was forced to climb higher into the forest. In the late afternoon, whilst cutting a path back down towards the river she came across a part of the forest that opened up into a glade, leading down to the water's edge. Knowing that it would soon be getting dark, she decided to set up camp there for the night.

She collected wood and built another fire. Once it was lit, she sat by it eating the rest of the fish she'd caught that morning and watching as the daylight faded and the stars came out. Aife found herself wondering if her father had ever made it this far downriver when he'd travelled as a young man. Certainly no-one else from her settlement would have. The outliers that they traded with were all either further inland or higher in the mountains above them. She might be the first person in the entire history of her settlement to have ever journeyed so far downriver and strangely that thought brought her some comfort as she sat there, looking up at the night sky.

She woke at first light. The fire was still smouldering slightly, so she added some fresh wood to it and got it going properly again. It had occurred to her the night before that she might be able to cut down a few of the young poplar trees in the glade, tie them together with some of the fabric from her clothes and make a small raft. It wouldn't be as sturdy as the skiff and she would have to stick closer to the bank, but at least her progress downriver might be a bit quicker. She fished with the spear again in the shallows, with less success than the day before and then began to investigate the glade for suitable trees to make the raft with.

Aife knew that to make a raft you needed a relatively light wood, as that would float better. Ideally, she knew that it would be better to take the wood from trees that have already been cut and allowed to dry so that some of the moisture has evaporated, but she didn't have that luxury. Slightly up the hill from where she'd made camp, she found what she was looking for: a group of young poplar trees, all approximately the same diameter. She cut down five using her father's sword and then hacked off the top branches and foliage before rolling and pushing them back down the hill to the camp. Then she set about removing any further knots or branches before cutting and dividing them into 6 foot logs. She left two of them slightly longer to create the connecting logs that would run the length of the raft. It was hard work, even with the help of the sharp sword, but by midday she was ready to begin building the raft.

Taking off her day gown, she laid it out flat on a large stone and cut it lengthwise into long strips. Then, floating the connecting logs out into the shallow water, she tied them together with two of the shorter logs, using the fabric from her gown to create the basic frame. Using fabric, instead of leather or rope, made things trickier, but eventually she was able to get the logs to hold together, tightly. She then added the other 'floater' logs to the frame, one by one. When she was finished, she was able to drag the raft close enough to the bank to make sure it didn't float away and created a makeshift punt, using a long thin branch which she'd cut off one of the trees, so at least she could steer it a little.

Once the raft was completed, she gathered what was left of her things and set off downriver. She kept close to the riverbank, as she was concerned that the raft might flip over if she wasn't careful, so her progress was slower than it had been in the skiff. Sticking to the shallows meant she also had to use the punt more often, not just because the current was weaker but also to avoid rushes or large stones near the bank edge. However, it was still faster than walking and even in the few hours of daylight she had left to her after spending most of the day on the raft's construction, she reckoned she'd covered at least as much distance as she had on foot the day before.

Having learnt her lesson not to try and pursue her journey in failing light, when she spotted a suitable-looking inlet in the late afternoon she punted her way to the bank and made her camp there for the night. The fishing was much better at this new spot and she was able to catch plenty to eat and even had enough to pack some surplus in the little pouch.

(4)

Matthew closed the door of the storage room behind him. He fumbled for the light switch and, when he found it, a strip of fluorescents blinked into life above his head. The room was about thirty metres square and filled with lockable cages where the residents could store their stuff.

He glanced through the wire mesh into the nearest cage and could see nothing except stacks of cardboard boxes and a couple of dining room chairs. He looked at the photos of the dig once again. From what he could make out, it seemed that it had extended all the way to the far wall as well as about a metre into the farthest cages on the right-hand side. Matthew made his way slowly along the row, looking into each of the cages as he passed. There was nothing special in any of them. He paused by the last two and looked inside more carefully but there was little more than cardboard boxes, a bicycle and a few other bits of old junk that the owners didn't want cluttering up their apartments.

Disappointed but largely unsurprised that his search had turned up nothing after all, Matthew was about to head back to the door when he felt a cold draft of air from behind him. He turned around and looked at the back wall of the storage room once more, wondering where on earth the draft might be coming from. Then he put out his hand to touch the wall and promptly disappeared from view.

Aife began her journey early the next day, aiming to travel as far as she could before nightfall. By noon, the intense brightness of the late summer sun reflecting off the water made her eyes and head ache. She directed the raft further into the shallows so that she might receive a bit shade from the trees that hung over the riverbank. Cupping out her hand to gather water from the river, she happened to glance up and saw something glinting through the trees of the forest, just up ahead. She punted closer to the bank and found a place where she could pull it on land. She could still make out the glinting object in the forest above her and climbed the hill to get a better look.

The object was further up the hillside than it seemed from the river's edge but, finally, the trees opened into a small clearing and there it was: a large archway, about 12 metres high and about a metre wide, made from highly polished stone. The archway rose to slight point (which was what she had seen from the river) rather being than completely round and in the centre there was a carved spiral. It stood alone in the clearing with no other signs of a structure or support anywhere near. The ground around and underneath it was completely flat, with none of the tell-tale signs of buildings or monuments that have fallen and been buried by the earth over time. There were a few patches of moss near the bottom and vines and bracken grew over and around parts of it, suggesting it had stood there for a long time and yet the parts of the white stone that shone through and glinted in the sun looked as brilliant as if they had been polished only hours before.

She walked all round the arch, to see if there was any form of inscription but there wasn't. Then she remembered where she'd seen that spiral before: She drew her father's sword and looked at the symbol engraved on the hilt - it was the same. Then she stepped through the archway and disappeared from view.

To Aife, it was as if she had just stepped into the mouth of a dark cave. Suddenly, she was in darkness. The floor underneath her leather shoes now felt much harder than earth. When she bent down to touch it, she found that it was made of some kind of metal. As she stood up again, she found her eyes beginning to adjust to the darkness. Whatever this space was, it extended back at least another twenty feet.

She heard a soft whirring sound and to her left dozens of small lights of different colours blinked into life. Aife stared at this strange sight, transfixed. She had never seen such a variety of colours, even in the most beautiful piece of pottery or jewellery. More importantly, these colours seemed to illuminate themselves from within, as if tiny flames burned inside them, making them even more brilliant. She put her hand out towards them, expecting to feel the warmth of whatever fire lay behind the colours, but instead found them cold and hard to the touch.

Looking at the lights more closely she saw that they each had black symbols on them, though she had no idea what they meant. The five largest lights were coloured red, blue, green, yellow and purple. Each of these had only a single symbol on them. The first red one looked like a straight vertical line, with a smaller line protruding from the top on the left and another slightly longer horizontal one at its base. The second blue button looked a little like a symbol for a river, curving down to the left until it bent off sharply to the right at the bottom. The green looked like a crude, half-finished drawing of a person or at least the body and the head - a smaller half circle on top of a larger one. Staring at the symbol for a moment, Aife also realised that it slightly resembled a person's bottom and surprised herself by laughing out loud. Now that she was standing closer to the lights, she could discern 5 more symbols written above the larger lights but not illuminated. The first and last were similar to that written on the large blue light, in that they too could be drawings of a river or water. It occurred to her that the five symbols written above the lights and the ones on the lights themselves might be connected. She took a step backwards and looked at all the symbols together. This is what she saw:

ZONES
1 2 3 4 5

Though she was still unable to understand what the symbols meant, it was now clear to her that the two sets were somehow connected to one another in meaning. Was it her imagination or did the yellow light with symbol on it seem slightly brighter than the others? She put her hand on it and felt it sink slightly under the weight of her palm. It was designed to be pressed! She tried pressing the blue light and noticed that it now burned brighter than the rest. Then she pressed the yellow button once more. Underneath the larger lights were more symbols that weren't illuminated. As she ran her fingers over them, she discovered a small black dial on the left hand side of the symbols. It twisted in her hand with a click and she saw the symbols next to it change slightly. She noticed there were further smaller dials under some of the other symbols. She twisted several of these to the right once or twice and saw the symbols above them change as well.

Just then something made her blood run cold: There was a sound like water being swirled and light flooded in from the other end of the chamber. Somebody or something had come in the other side. Aife ran back out the way she had come in. The daylight in the clearing was dazzling in comparison to the darkened chamber, but Aife continued on down the hillside, her eyes watering against the light. She stumbled a couple of times and eventually slipped over onto her back and slid the last few feet down the hill. At last, she came to the place where she'd left the raft and instantly let out a wail.

It was nowhere to be seen.

She scoured the riverbank to see if it had drifted further along but there was no trace of it whatsoever. Then she heard the sound of something coming down the hillside behind her. Frantic, she dove into the river and swam out into the middle of the current and let it take her along. She tried to swim a little but her woollen clothes quickly took on water and she soon found that she needed all her energy just to keep her head above the surface. She couldn't have looked back even if she'd wanted to. If she had, she would have seen the man with the scarred face who watched her from the riverbank as she struggled against the current.

[6]

Like Aife, Matthew found himself inside the darkened portal as the control panel slowly illuminated. For a few seconds he thought he might be in another part of the basement, but that thought quickly evaporated when he remembered that he'd managed to walk through a solid wall.

He moved closer to the panel and looked at the controls. Unlike Aife, he had no trouble understanding their meaning, for they were all written in English. At the top, there was a display showing the current year, month, day, hour, minute and second. However, this wasn't a year based on the Gregorian calendar or even the Hebrew one. Whoever had designed this device had based the year calculations on some Holocene form of time measurement and, as such, there was no delineation between A.D. and B.C. and the current year was a far bigger number than he was used to. Below that were the illuminated buttons showing each of the zones that had so puzzled Aife and finally the controls to set what moment in time you wished to travel to.

Even with the evidence in front of his eyes, Matthew could scarcely believe what he was looking at.

There was no doubt about it - this was a time machine.

Someone had actually managed to build one! Somehow it must also exist outside of the actual physical moment he had come from, in some sort of temporal bubble, because what other explanation was there that he had walked through a solid wall to enter it and that this portal, or whatever it was, had been undisturbed by the building of the apartment block. Matthew's brain struggled to cope with the implications of this last thought, but it was the only option that made any sense. Somehow, neither the residents, the teams of builders or even his father and the team of archeologists who had been digging here, had discovered it - even thought many of them would have been standing right next to it. How was that possible?

Looking up at the top of the control panel gave Matthew the answer. There, embossed into the metal, was a familiar looking symbol of a spiral. That was it - the sword was the key to the portal! Only if you came to the location of the portal with the sword would you be able to enter. The thought that his own father had probably stood next to an actual time machine, without ever realising it, made Matthew chuckle for a moment before the full realisation of what that actually meant stopped his amusement dead it its tracks.

The sword had been buried at the same level as the other bronze age artefacts.

That meant the portal had been here since the bronze age - before that even, if the numbering of the years in the portal were anything to go by. How many had known of this secret? And how had the portals gotten there to begin with? They had a modern number system and yet they had existed in the past. How was that even possible unless some future beings had gone back into the past, created the portal and left it there?

I'll ask them, Matthew thought and, turning the large dial to the right, spun himself forward fifty years into the future.

chapter four:
encounters &
discoveries

ife was extremely lucky. After a few minutes travelling downriver, she came across a large branch floating in the water that she was able to cling onto and keep herself afloat. She wouldn't have been able to keep her head above water much longer otherwise. After floating along on the branch for some time, she noticed that the sun was beginning to slip behind the trees on her right. She needed to find a place to make camp for the night. She spotted a suitable looking part of the bank which tapered down gently towards the water and with trees that were far enough back from the water's edge to enable her to make a camp there. She kicked hard with her legs and tried to steer the branch towards the bank, but to no avail. So she slid off it and swam as hard as she could. It took almost all of her remaining strength to do so and once she made it to the bank she lay there in the mud, exhausted, for some time.

It was starting to get dark by the time she began searching for wood to make a fire. She gathered together as much dry wood as she could find and lit the fire quickly, before night set in completely. She got as near to fire as she could and rubbed herself to keep warm. It was too dark to fish, but fortunately she still had some of the food she'd caught that morning. She was too tired to eat much though and after a few mouthfuls, lay down next to the fire and fell asleep.

[2]

Matthew let go of the dial and looked at the new date. Fifty years into the future. He would be 65 by now. He picked up his rucksack with the sword and left the portal once more.

He found himself ankle deep in water. He was still in the basement of the apartment block but there wasn't much left of it. The stairs that had previously led up to the ground floor, now led to open grey skies. and the ruins of what once had been the building. Matthew climbed the steps carefully, dodging the rumble strewn across them and tried to avoid touching the walls which were covered with large bugs.

Almost as soon as he was out in the open, he had trouble breathing properly. The sky was grey black and the air thick with smog and particles, making visibility poor. He could just about make out the shape of the sun through the pollution in the atmosphere, though it seemed to give off little in the way of light or heat. Gasping for air, he took the scarf from around his neck and fastened it over his nose and mouth. This helped a little. He looked out across the desolate grey landscape. Many of the buildings had gone or stood in ruins. The earth looked waterlogged and in places had frozen. There was no birdsong and all the trees were bare. The whole are seemed devoid of any kind of life. There was no movement of any kind, save for the wind which whistled through the cracks in the buildings.

Out of the corner of his eye, Matthew caught sight of something moving in the upstairs window of the building opposite. He turned his head just in time to catch a glimpse of a figure before they ducked out of sight.

"Hey!" he called out, but there was no reply.

Matthew made his way over to the building, which had probably been worth a small fortune in an affluent neighbourhood such as this, but which now resembled a haunted house from an old film. All the windows were smashed or cracked and the front door hung crooked on its hinges. It creaked loudly as Matthew pushed it open.

"Hallo?" Once again his voice was met with deafening silence.

Matthew walked over to the foot of the staircase and looked up. From the second floor, the grimy face of a young girl stared back at him for a few seconds and then was gone.

"Hey, don't be afraid!" he called after her, "I won't hurt you."

He started moving slowly up the stairs, trying to avoid touching the walls which, like the basement, were covered with all manner of insects. He stopped every now and then, looking to see if the young girl would show her face again but she didn't. He reached the first floor. Most of the windows had been boarded up on this side of the house and the little daylight that shone through the gaps didn't extend very far into any of the rooms. He stood there on the first floor landing, listening for a moment, but heard nothing other than the wind whistling through the cracks in the boards.

He stood on the first step of the next set of stairs and looked up towards the second floor. There was the grimy faced girl once more. She couldn't be more than 8 years old.

"There you are...don't run off again, I won't hurt you," Matthew said. "What's your name?"

The grimy faced little girl tilted her head slightly and stared at Matthew in a slightly quizzical way, but didn't answer.

"Are you here all by yourself? Where's your family?"

The little girl shook her head and smiled.

Suddenly, several pairs of hands grabbed Matthew by his arms and legs and yanked him away from the stairs, so that he fell with a thud onto the floor of the landing. Almost immediately, flurries of blows landed on his chest, arms and legs and Matthew was forced to put his hands up to protect his face. Then, there was a loud bang. The attack stopped and he heard several pairs of footsteps scurrying away from him. Taking his hands away from his face he looked up to see the man with the scarred face, holding out his hand towards him.

"You're the man from my dream," was all Matthew could think to say.

"My name is Morfran and it's not safe to stay here. I've scared them off for now, but they'll soon be back, armed and in greater numbers. We need to leave."

Morfran's voice was muffled and slightly metallic. In the half light of the shadowy landing Matthew could just about make out that he had some sort of mask or breathing apparatus over his nose and mouth.

"Come on!" Morfran repeated, "we need to get back to the portal." He grabbed Matthew's arm and pulled him to his feet.

The two of them moved quickly back downstairs and out the front door. Outside, Matthew could see that they were no longer alone. From several of the ruined buildings nearby, people in tattered clothes were emerging, many of them had wooden clubs or old pieces of metal that had been fashioned into crude, machete-type weapons. Morfran pushed Matthew forward and the two of them raced back towards the steps that led back down into the basement where the portal was. Matthew was aware that the ragged figures from the other buildings were following them.

As they reached the bottom of the basement steps, a figure lunged at them from out of the shadows, welding a large, steel table leg. Morfran was able to push Matthew out of the way just in time and leg struck the wall instead. He drew what looked like a small pistol from his belt and fired it at their assailant. The resulting blast of light illuminated the entire basement for a few seconds and Matthew could make out a few more ragged figures huddled in the shadows. Morfran pulled Matthew to his feet and the two of them ran forward towards the wall. When they were both inside the portal again, Matthew sank to his knees, exhausted.

"Who are you and who were those people?" he gasped, as he removed the scarf from over his nose and mouth. "Why were they trying to kill us?"

Those people back there were scavengers," Morfran replied, "and don't take it personally - they'd kill anyone who they thought had something they needed. Food and clothing are in short supply. I don't imagine they'd seen clothes as nice as yours for a very long time. As for me, I'm here to help you, Matthew, that's all you need to know."

"Then it was lucky, you came along when you did..."

"Luck didn't have much to do with it - but you'll need to be more careful. You can't just go travelling blindly through time, without taking any sort of precautions."

"I see that now," Matthew replied, "I just didn't expect anything like that...what the hell happened back there? It looked like the aftermath of a nuclear war or something..."

"Nothing so dramatic. Climate change, flash floods, heavy storms, combined with large scale pandemics managed to be apocalyptic enough on their own, without the need for nuclear armageddon. This is just what happens when the average temperature of the world rises by 4 degrees."

"But I thought we were dealing with climate change? Electric cars, recycling plastic bags, offsetting carbon footprints, wind farms..."

"Yes, it just wasn't enough. We still couldn't completely give up fossil fuels or plastics, so the damage continued and by the time the richest and most powerful people in the world finally took the problem seriously, it was too late."

"And this is what's left then? This is what humanity's future looks like - returning to being murderous savages with ruined buildings instead of caves?"

"Only here. It's different all over the world. Those living here are moderately fortunate - they only need to cope with starvation due to droughts during the summer and frozen winters when nothing can grow - the hottest places became deserts, forests burnt all year round and coastal areas are now underwater. Anyone with money escaped long ago, out into space - leaving their mess behind, for those less fortunate to have to deal with."

"Is there a way to stop it?"

"There might be...if the right person was up to the task..."

"Me? But I wouldn't even know where to start...are you really telling me that I alone have to save the world?"

"Not alone, no. Everyone has to do their part, but some people are better situated to make change happen faster than others. Thanks to your father's money, you have financial resources; if you are to change the fate of the world that change would need to start from the moment you're from, perhaps even earlier, if you were to have any chance of success - for that you have the portal. Most important of all, to really change the fate of the planet you'd need a stockpile of something more valuable than even money - the means to store clean energy. After all, there are plenty of ideas as to how we could slow or even partially reverse the effects of climate change, but they all need to be powered in some way and whether through solar or wind power that energy still needs to be stored...do you understand?"

"The lepidolite!"

Morfran nodded. "Exactly. Your father was right - there must have been a mine nearby. The only natural deposit of it in these parts, untouched for thousands of years. Whoever finds it would have a considerable natural resource for producing lithium, which essential for any sort of rechargeable energy storage - that's why the world's most powerful men and conglomerates want to control it. You're already wealthy, so you don't need to make money off of the lithium. Once the mine is up and running it will pay for itself and you can re-invest the profits in other initiatives to help reverse climate change. That's important - otherwise you're just another rich idiot making money by raping the earth and we have enough of those already. The profits and the lithium you produce must only be used to support green projects and push the world back from the brink. By doing this, you will also automatically become powerful and influential - which you can use to your advantage to exert political pressure on the government and other organisations to make sure the change actually happens. However, first you need to find the mine."

"You don't know where it is?"

"No, that's the problem. We might be standing on top of it right now. Over the last three thousand or so years since the bronze age, that knowledge was lost and the mine was forgotten, but it must be somewhere nearby otherwise why would it have been found near a portal? It would be almost impossible to find it now, but if someone were to locate it in the past and fix its co-ordinates, it could still be found at any point in time."

"But why not use the portal to find it yourself?"

"I did try, a long time ago. Now someone younger needs to take up the challenge..."

"But why me?"

Morfran simply smiled. "All that will become apparent, in time... You will need something to fix the co-ordinates of the mine - one of these to be exact..." He held out a small black box with display on it.

"What is it?"

"A quantum compass. Something that relies on G.P.S. will be useless in a time before satellites existed, obviously, but this measures the relative position of something using atom interferometry. It was originally developed to detect the position of things that can't use traditional satellite navigation, a fully submerged submarine for example. It can also convert that information into G.P.S. co-ordinates."

"I had no idea something like that even existed..."

"That's not terribly surprising. In your time, handheld units like this one are barely out of the prototype stage. Fortunately, the company that makes them are local and looking for investors for their final stage of funding to get the units into production. You'll need to get in touch with them, invest heavily and get your hands on a prototype."

"Why can't you simply give me one from the future?"

"It doesn't work like that Matthew. If I did, I'd be changing the past. Then the future, my present would be different. You'd do well to remember that, when you're travelling through time: any changes in the past effect the future - so be careful what you change and who you interact with." He held out the device to

Matthew once more and showed him the name of the manufacturer. "This is the company, make sure you remember the name."

"But this is ridiculous, even with this device I still don't even know where or when to start looking…"

"The mine must be somewhere near one of the portals."

"You mean there's more than one?"

"Of course," Morfran replied and indicated the Zone buttons on the control panel. "There are five, spread at intervals throughout this area, all interlinked with each other. Pressing any of the Zone buttons takes you immediately to that particular portal, whilst still remaining in the same point of time that you're currently in."

"So they're a teleportation device as well as a time machine?"

"Exactly."

"How wide an area do the portals cover?"

"It's large, but not so large as to make the journeys between them impossible. I suggest you find out for yourself - in your own time, though, not anyone else's. It'll help you to keep your bearings when you're in other times as well. In earlier times, the portals were marked by an archway, but over time those were destroyed. You would be well advised to mark their position with the quantum compass as well, so that you can always find them and whatever happens…" he tapped Matthew's backpack containing the sword, "don't lose your key. Otherwise you'll be trapped in whatever time you're in."

He turned to the control panel and twisted the dial to the left until it reached the moment that Matthew had left.

"Be sure to note the time and date from which you travelled, as well," Morfran said, "that way you can always find your way back to moment in time that you came from. This is where I have to leave you, I'm afraid."

"But I still have questions..." Matthew said, as Morfran ushered him towards the entrance of the portal.

"You'll figure out the answers yourself, in time. It's been good to see you Matthew, please take better care of yourself in the future though...and in the past, for that matter."

"Will I ever see you again?"

"Who knows..."

With that he gently pushed Matthew through the portal entrance and Matthew found himself, once more, in the basement of the apartment block.

[3]

Aife awoke to the sound of something moving nearby. She had no idea how long she'd slept for. The fire had died down a little, making it difficult to see much in the gloom. She heard movement again, seemingly just beyond the circle of firelight this time. Aife drew her father's sword. She would be ready for it, whatever it was. She saw something white move a few feet in front of her and heard a low growl. The face of large white wolf appeared out of the darkness, illuminated by the flickering firelight. She cautiously moved herself 'round, so that the fire was between her and the wolf and listened carefully for further movement on either side of her, in case other wolves were surrounding her, but could hear nothing. Either the others were very quiet or this wolf was alone.

As her settlement had kept pigs and sheep, Aife had grown up knowing all about wolves. Now and again, wolves would try and steal livestock or even leftover food from the settlement, but they almost never posed a threat to humans themselves. The lone wolf, generally an older female wolf who had been driven from the pack, could present a threat, however. Not being in a pack, they had difficulty hunting and could try and kill anything if they were hungry enough.

Aife watched as the wolf came closer to the fire. She could now see her fur was totally white aside for some grey on the tail and on its forepaws. Her ears were flattened back and through the light of the fire Aife could see that the wolf's amber eyes were narrowed. She bared her fangs at Aife and growled softly once more. Aife lowered the sword slightly and pulled some of the food she had saved from the pouch she had around her waist. The wolf's expression changed immediately she saw the food. Her eyes widened and her ears came up. She tracked Aife's hand attentively as she moved the food back and forth. Then she threw it into the air and it hit the ground just behind the wolf, who turned and gobbled it up immediately.

The wolf turned her attention back to Aife once more, but this time the ears remained up and the amber eyes looked hopeful.

She wants more, Aife thought.

She pulled another piece of fish from the pouch and began the same process again but this time, the wolf backed up slightly and caught the food neatly in her jaws. She swallowed the fish almost without chewing it at all and looked at Aife once more.

She decided to try something. Taking another piece of fish from the pouch she slowly moved around the fire so that it was no longer between her and the wolf, holding out the piece of fish in her hand as she did so. The wolf instantly backed away and flattened her ears, distrustful again. Aife crouched down slightly and made a slow and elaborate show of putting the sword on the ground, keeping eye contact with the wolf the entire time. With the sword lying next to her, she extended her hand out still further but the wolf made no step forwards. Aife threw the piece of fish on the floor a few feet away from her and sat back on her heels. The wolf, still eying Aife suspiciously, slowly made her way forward to the piece of fish on the ground. She stretched out her body and ate it without taking her eyes off of Aife the whole time. Then she licked her lips and looked at Aife inquisitively. Aife slowly removed another piece of fish from the pouch and held it out, palm upwards, towards the wolf. This time she came forwards slowly and after sniffing Aife's hand briefly, took the piece of fish gently from her hand and backed away a few steps and lay on the ground and ate it between her paws.

Once she was done she stood up again and now moved slowly towards Aife. She took another piece of fish from the pouch and held it in her hand once more, but this time keeping her arm close to her, rather than stretching it out. The wolf came to Aife and took the fish from her hand, allowing Aife to gently stroke the fur around her head as she did so. Then she settled down next to Aife as if they had been friends for life. As she fed the wolf the last few remaining pieces of fish, the animal became more and more at ease with her, eating contentedly whilst she stroked her fur. When the fish was finished, Aife let her sniff the pouch, so she understood there was nothing more to eat. The wolf licked Aife's fingers and then her own paws and settled her head on Aife's lap.

"What shall I call you?" she said aloud to the wolf as she lay heavily on her lap and allowed Aife to fondle her ears. "How about Fionn? Traditionally, it's a boy's name, but it can be used for a girl as well. In my language it means white, but it can also mean something true or sincere... Are you true, now, Fionn? Or will you simply eat me as soon as I fall asleep?"

Fionn raised her head slightly and as if in response to this question, uttered a sound that was a cross between a yawn and a sigh and then closed her eyes once more. Aife tried to stay awake as long as she could, but eventually her eyelids began to grow heavy and she lay down next to Fionn and fell asleep too.

(4)

Matthew became a major investor in the fledgling company producing quantum compasses and they were only too happy to lend him a prototype, which he told them he was planning to test on an archeological dig. This also had the additional benefit of impressing his various business managers, who praised his savvy in wanting to invest in what was surely to be an important new technology. Once he'd managed to get hold of a prototype, Matthew began to explore the different zones in his own time, just as Morfran had suggested. To make things easier, he persuaded Weston to let him use the family's penthouse apartment in the block itself, so he now longer needed to worry about how he got in the front door.

He decided to begin with Zone 4, the next nearest to his own and work backwards, gradually moving further away from where he started. Unbeknownst to Matthew, this was also the same zone that Aife had stumbled across, though it looked very different in his time. Gone was the clearing of trees and the archway itself, that had stood on the small hill over looking the river. Gone too was the river, in fact, as the flow of water which fed it which had long since been dammed and diverted further upstream creating a large valley through which a great many houses had been built.

Stepping through the portal in Zone 4, Matthew found himself in a cramped but immaculately organised space, surrounded by various tools which he realised must be a garden shed of some kind. Sure enough, a glance through the small window at the side of the shed, confirmed that he was in the garden of a row of neat upmarket houses. He silently thanked his good fortune that the owner of the shed was so compulsively tidy. If the shed had been as disorganised as the one at home, he would have no doubt been crushed by the weight of sundry tools and other junk falling on him as soon as he stepped through the portal. It also made him realise that it would be better to enter and exit the various portals at night to avoid the possibility of being seen. He used the quantum compass to measure the exact position of the entrance to the portal for future reference and then went back inside it.

The benefit of being inside a portal through space and time meant Matthew didn't need to wait until it got dark to continue his exploration of the portals, he simply set the controls a few hours ahead and moved on to the next zone.

Zone 3 let out into a concrete carpark. Matthew cautiously made his way through to the exit and discovered he was in the grounds of a health spa, higher up the valley from the previous Zone. Worried that he might be seen by member of staff, he headed back towards the portal entrance but quickly had to duck behind one of the concrete pillars when he almost walked into a man and a woman who were having a conversation next to one of the parked cars.

"...it's not that I mind having to pull a double shift now and again, it just seems to have become the norm, lately," said the woman, who constantly fingered her car keys as she spoke.

"Maybe you should take some of the overtime you've accumulated, and just have a week off..." the man, whom Matthew guessed was probably some form of security guard, replied.

"Fat chance of that happening, Joe! Not with Mel on maternity leave at the moment. Sheila's not going to give anyone any time off."

"Yeah, I suppose you're right. Hey, what about coming out tomorrow night after work? Sam, Julie and me were planning to have a few drinks and try out that new Thai restaurant that's opened in town."

"Tomorrow's no good, I'm afraid," the woman replied. "I promised my sister that I'd drop off some old clothes of Maggie's that should fit her daughter now and to be honest, after the week I've had, I'll probably just end up going home to bed afterwards."

"Ok, Sue, some other time then ..."

"Sure, I'd like that..."

Good, now get in the car and drive off, thought Matthew.

Clearly Sue had other ideas though, and as she was halfway into her car, she suddenly thought of something and called out to Joe.

"Hey, what happened about that other job you applied for?".

"Still not heard anything..." Joe replied, walking back towards her.

Matthew sighed. These two were clearly not going anywhere anytime soon and every minute waiting for them to leave increased the risk that someone might come towards the carpark from the opposite direction and see him. He needed to get back to the portal. If he could just get past both of them, then the other parked cars would probably hide him the rest of the way. There were some loose stones by the path leading from the car park, behind him. He chose a medium sized one and threw it towards the far end of the car park. He'd been aiming for the ground but his throw was poor and it hit the bonnet of a car with a bang that the concrete walls reverberated into a much bigger sound.

"What the hell was that?!" Sue asked, flinching at the noise.

With their attention momentarily directed towards the other end of the carpark, Matthew, crouching as low as he could, moved around the back of the pillar and hurried towards the nearest parked car.

"Just stay there while I take a look..." Joe replied and moved towards the spot where the noise had come from.

As he did so, Matthew moved quietly from one parked car to the next and then, checking that they were both looking in the opposite direction, crossed over to the other side. Once he was safely behind the parked car next to the portal. He quickly took out the quantum compass from his pocket and made a note of the portal's location before crawling back to it as quietly as possible.

That had been far too close for comfort.

(5)

When Aife awoke the sky was bright and there was no sign of Fionn. The fire had burnt down to nothing and she felt quite cold in the morning air. She gathered some fresh wood for the fire and cut a new spear for fishing from the branch of a nearby tree. Then she waded out into the river a short distance and set about catching as many fish as she could manage, just in case her new friend returned. Once she felt she'd caught enough, she cooked them over the newly remade fire. Just as the fish were almost done she heard a rustle in the trees behind her and Fionn re-appeared with a hare in her mouth.

"Oh have you brought something for our feast too?," Aife asked, as the wolf carefully dropped the hare's carcass next to her. Aife reached slowly for the hare's lifeless body, watching Fionn the whole time, worried that the wolf might change her mind about letting Aife have a share of her kill. Aife threw down some of the fish for the wolf who gobbled it up hungrily. Taking her father's sword, Aife neatly gutted the hare and threw the intestines to Fionn as well, before skinning it. She roasted it over the fire using a long stick as a makeshift spit. Though it wasn't a particularly large hare, with the addition of the fish they had more than enough to eat and Aife was able to pack some of the leftovers into her pouch once more.

There seemed little point in trying to construct another raft as there was very little suitable wood near the camp and with Fionn seemingly happy to accompany her, Aife continued the journey on foot. It was almost noon by the time they began and the going was slow as the trees and bushes were dense there by the water's edge. After a few hours, Aife stopped to rest on a log for a few moments and Fionn, having caught the scent of something on the breeze, went off through the trees quietly. Aife waited sometime for the wolf to return and then decided to continue on, figuring that Fionn would probably be able to track her and find her if she wanted to. Sure enough, a little while later Fionn re-appeared from the trees, her white fur bloody and carrying the leg of a deer in her mouth as a gift for Aife.

Finding a suitable place to make camp shortly afterwards, Aife built a fire and roasted the deer leg over it. Sharing it and the leftover food from the morning with Fionn.

Over the next few days, this became a familiar routine for the two of them. Aife would try and catch some fish as soon as it was light so at least they had something to eat and Fionn would often come back from an early morning hunt with a rabbit or a fox. Once she brought back a badger, which Aife had never seen before and after tasting a little, decided she would leave most of it for Fionn. Once done with eating, they would continue their journey along the riverbank once more. Sometimes Fionn would catch the scent of something and disappear off, whilst Aife continued on by herself. If Fionn couldn't find or catch whatever it was that she'd smelt on the breeze, she normally returned to Aife fairly quickly. Whereas if she took longer, Aife came to realise, it was because she'd managed to hunt and kill whatever it was and would eat her fill of the carcass before bringing something back for Aife, just as she might for the cubs in a pack.

On the fourth day, the change in the weather coincided with the beginning of Aife's monthly 'days'. The cramps were severe this time and it was clear to her that, with the pain, she would be unlikely to make much progress that day.

She managed to form a shelter for herself against the rain, using some cut branches. After she'd arranged the shelter she made a fire at the opening to keep warm. She found some large stones down by the water's edge when she washed herself and warmed them over the fire, before wrapping them carefully in the remains of her cloak and holding them against her stomach to alleviate the pain.

Fionn brought her part of a kill in the middle of the afternoon, which she ate gladly, as she was in no condition to fish for anything today. Despite her using cloth cut from her cloak to stem the bleeding, she had been worried that the smell of blood might make it unsafe for her to be around the wolf, but if Fionn noticed the smell she showed no sign of it effecting her loyalty towards Aife. She wondered in those idle moments whether the wolf's heightened sense of smell might be able to distinguish a difference between one type of bleeding or another and whether being female herself, she was able to identify it for what it was.

Aife thought back to the first time, some years before, when she started to menstruate. She'd felt unwell most of that morning and believed at first that she eaten something that hadn't agreed with her. It was only when she'd noticed the blood, midway through the morning whilst helping Idelisa with some chores, that she realised what was happening.

She'd returned home at once to clean herself up and make preparations (as was the custom) to stay in the birthing house for the duration of her period. When she informed her father, he surprised her by suggesting that she stay at home instead, and just rest until her menstruation was over.

"I feel a responsibility, you see Aife..." he explained. "Normally, your mother would be here to guide and support you during this important moment in your life and accompany you to the birthing house. As she isn't, I feel I should be there for you in her place. If I send you away, I will miss this important part of my daughter's journey to becoming an adult and I don't want you to be alone this first time. I asked Nareena for some advice as to what remedies might help with the pain and she was very helpful. So, if you wish to stay here instead, I will take care of you."

Once again, this was her father breaking with tradition. Women were viewed as unclean during the days of their menstruation and many men in the settlement felt they could not share the same space, let alone accept food, from the hands of their wives and daughters during this time. It had often seemed to Aife that many of the women accepted this custom purely because they were only too glad to spend a few days away from their menfolk, in the company of other women in the birthing house.

Her father made it clear that it was her choice, of course, and if she preferred to go the birthing house then she was welcome to do so. In the end, Aife, elected to stay home that first time and her father, true to his word, looked after her - though she suspected it caused enormous uproar amongst the council members for him to do so. To spare her father further problems, she'd gone to the birthing house every time since and whilst she too had enjoyed the opportunity to chat with her friends and the other women of the settlement, she'd also enjoyed the time alone with her father and the talks they had had together.

The pain had subsided a little by the evening and as she felt quite tired, she lay down in the shelter next to Fionn and tried to sleep a little. When she awoke sometime later it was pitch black and raining heavily once more. She could hear the occasional crack of thunder and just then the whole sky was lit up by a flash of lightning. The fire had died down almost completely and she could hear Fionn growling softly between the thunderclaps.

"Don't worry, silly," she said stroking the wolf's ears, "it's only thunder."

But Fionn remained tense and alert. Listening more closely now, Aife also began to detect another sound separate from the noise of the storm, that she had initially taken for the howl of the wind amongst the trees. However, as the howl grew in volume she suddenly discerned what it was and why Fionn had begun to growl in those few seconds before the roof of her shelter was suddenly torn away and a hairy black shape blotted out the sky above. She just had time to register the bear's hot, rancid breath on her face before Fionn pounced, knocking the animal backwards and into the open ground by the embers of the fire. Aife grabbed the sword and pushed her way out of what remained of her shelter to stand her ground next to Fionn, who already had her hackles raised and her teeth bared in readiness for the bear's next attack.

The lightning split the sky once more and now Aife got her first proper glimpse of the huge animal, lumbering towards them once more. Although Fionn's retaliation had taken it by surprise, it had recovered quickly and now it had discovered the source of sweet, bloody scent that excited its nostrils, it would move on them again.

Aife's experience with bears had been minimal as they rarely came close to a large settlement such as hers, but further towards the outlier settlements the risk of running into one was much greater and as such, she like the other children, had been taught what to do if they encountered one:

Never turn and run. Bears are much faster than their bulk might suggest. Turning and running will trigger the same "rush instinct" that all large predators share. The bear will chase you down easily and tear you apart.

Stand your ground and make yourself as "big" as you can. Bears can be scared off if their prey seems larger and more aggressive than they are.

If you have to fight, fix and lower your position with your weapon (preferably something long like a spear) in front of you and skewer the animal as it attacks you, using its own weight to drive the point as deep as possible.

Aife knelt next to the sharpened branch that she'd cut in order to fish with. She picked it up slowly from its place by the fire, never taking her eyes from the bear for a second. The bear roared as she did so and Fionn snarled at the creature once more.

"Come on then!" she shouted at the bear, once she had the spear in one hand and the sword in the other. "If you want to try and kill me, get on with it! Don't take all night!"

She stood up and stretching her arms out as wide as she could, roared at the bear with all her might, trying to make herself as intimidating as possible. The bear seemed to back away for a second before rising up on its haunches and roaring back at her. Its front paws came back to the ground with a crash and it immediately began charging towards her. Aife knelt down once more, jamming the spear into the ground in front of her. Fionn hit the bear side on, mid charge, but was swatted away again quickly. The wolf landed on the ground with a yelp but leapt to her feet again and jumped onto the bear's back, helping to push it onto the tip of the spear as it loomed over Aife. The bear howled in pain as the spear went into its chest and crashed on its right side, snapping the spear in two and dislodging Fionn once more as it did so. It tried to swipe at Aife with its left paw but only succeeded in connecting with the sword instead, howling once more as the blade bit cleanly into its flesh. Fionn clambered up on top of the beast and sunk her jaws into its jugular before Aife brought the sword crashing down in a wide arc and buried it deep in the animal's skull.

Exhausted, Aife dropped to the ground and sat there, whilst Fionn took her fill from the carcass. Once satisfied that she'd eaten enough for now, the wolf came over to Aife to make sure she was ok.

"Well, done girl..." Aife said, as she sat stroking the white wolf's fur which was now matted with the bear's blood. "No need to look for food tomorrow, we've got enough to keep us going for a while now."

The storm was no longer directly over head and the wind and rain had died down a little. Aife repaired the shelter as best she could and lay down once more underneath it. She slept quickly and when she next awoke, the rain had passed and bright sunshine shone down on what was left of the bear.

chapter five:
faces old & new

After his experience in Zone 3, Matthew was considerably more cautious when he visited the next two, crouching down and shuffling forward when exiting the portal and making sure he took a reading of the portal's location with the compass straight away, in case he needed to make a quick exit.

Fortunately, neither proved particularly hazardous.

Zone 2 opened into the storeroom of a large supermarket, which due to Matthew's arrival at nighttime was closed, whilst Zone 1 opened onto the playground of a public park. After wandering around the park a little, Matthew realised it was one he had visited several times as a child.

Later, whilst plotting the various locations of the portals on a walking map, Matthew came to realise just how far the distances between each of the portals were and how wide his search area was. Zone 1 was in the next county, high up in the hills. Even in a car, it was almost a day's drive away from where the apartment block stood. From there, the path of the portals descended down gradually to Zone 2 then zigzagged across to Zones 3 and 4 on the other side of the valley, before twisting back on itself slightly to Zone 5 underneath the apartment block like a misshapen 'S'.

The enormity of the task began to dawn on him for the first time. Searching this entire area during the bronze age could take him years, decades even. He would need to plan this carefully and try and narrow down the search a little. He looked at the map again. Zone 3 was high up on one side of the valley, judging by its topography alone, having a mine close to it seemed unlikely. That left 4 other zones. He looked up the locations of some of the well known lepidolite mines around the world on the Internet. Some were near lakes, like the one in Manitoba, Canada. Others were in mountainous terrain, such as one in the Ural Mountains in Russia. None of this gave him much of a clue where to start. Perhaps if he knew more about geology he'd have some idea, but at that moment his task was beginning to seem more and more like searching for a needle in a haystack - in fact, that sounded relatively simple by comparison.

He looked at the Wikipedia pages on lepidolite again. Not all lepidolite was the same colour. Some had a bright yellow hue, whilst other pieces were almost transparent. Rose coloured examples, like the one his father had found, had been mined in Virgem da Lapa, in Brazil. The city was on the bank of a river. Perhaps the mine he was searching for was similarly located. It wasn't much, but it was a start. He would start in Zone 1 and follow the flow of the water which came down from streams in the mountains and presumably back then had flowed right down through the valley. With a little bit of luck he might just find something.

[2]

Aife and Fionn spent the next two days in the same spot as Aife slowly skinned and washed the bear's pelt before drying it to make a cloak for herself, that would also double as a warm blanket once the nights grew colder. She also cooked up any of the meat that she felt was usable, even though she didn't find it particularly tasty, as it was important to have some supplies in reserve.

It was several hours after they'd been underway, once more, that Aife heard Fionn growling up ahead. Aife made her way through the trees following the sound. Slightly uphill and in land from the river, the trees became less dense and, up ahead, Aife could see Fionn tugging at something on the ground beside her. As Aife got closer she saw that Fionn had something in her mouth.

A piece of meat.

A piece of meat that was tied to one of the trees!

Fortunately, the deadfall had been set for something far heavier than either Aife or Fionn. Perhaps the very same bear that had attacked them. As it was, Aife felt the ground beneath her feet slowly begin to give and on instinct she threw herself to the side, striking out with her father's sword as she did so, managing to get a purchase on some solid ground before the branches and twigs covering the deadfall gave way and the bottom half of her torso was left dangling in midair. Fionn dropped the meat and ran over to Aife, taking hold of her sleeve and trying to help drag her away from the hole. With Fionn's help, Aife managed to pull her legs up and then lay panting on the mossy ground beside Fionn.

"That was a close one," she said as Fionn sniffed her intensely to make sure she wasn't hurt. "I might have known your stomach would get us into trouble sooner or later."

Fionn looked at her pityingly and gave a short yawn.

Having got her breath back, Aife sat up and looked down at the open deadfall. It was deep enough, that had she fallen in she would never have been able to get out unaided. That was assuming she hadn't been impaled on one of the large wooden stakes buried in the earth at the bottom of the pit.

"Humans made this," she said to Fionn. "That means there must be a settlement nearby."

[3]

It took Matthew a few days to gather together everything he needed for his trip into the past. As well as the sword, the quantum compass and the map he'd made of the portals in his own time, he packed a first aid kit with a cauterising suture, a good supply of refillable water bottles as well as packets of dried food and an ultra light sleeping bag. He was planning to set the controls in the portal to take him back to the bronze age during the middle of summer, so hopefully the weather would be relatively warm and he wouldn't get pneumonia if he had to sleep outside.

After considerable searching on the internet, he was able to piece together suitable clothing that, he hoped, wouldn't look too out of place in the time he was travelling to.

Finally he was ready. He'd gone over the map countless times, plotting distances to where he thought the course of the river might have run back then, so that at he least he would be travelling in the right direction. He went to bed early that night and slept until 10 the next day - knowing it might be his last night in a comfortable bed for some time.

[4]

Suspecting that any settlement would probably be based close to the water's edge, Aife and Fionn climbed higher up the hillside so there was less chance of wandering into the middle of the settlement's territory by accident. After all, she no reason to expect that they would automatically welcome a stranger into their midst, especially if accompanied by a large white wolf.

After making their way cautiously for some time, Fionn stopped suddenly and growled softly in the direction of the river. They headed down from the hillside and were soon able to see the settlement below them. Aife spotted a small stone ridge, a few yards to the left of them and there she crouched down next to Fionn to observe what was going on.

The settlement was smaller and the buildings were much simpler than those of her own. There was nothing as elaborate the many chambered council broch, here. Most of the dwellings were single storey roundhouses, similar to that of her Aunt and Uncle's. There seemed to be a wooden gangway leading to some other structures closer to the water's edge, but it was hard to make these out through the trees. All the settlement's animals, a few pigs and sheep mainly, were kept in pens in the centre of the group of huts and Aife could see some areas, near the edge of the settlement, where the forest had been cleared and the land ploughed in order to grow crops and vegetables.

The layout of the settlement and the close proximity of the animals and the crops made Aife think of the outliers who traded with her settlement. Like these people, the outlier settlements faced a far greater chance of attacks from bears or wolves (who seldom ventured too close to a large settlement such as her own), as well as far greater hardships should their crops fail. Here at least they had the added advantage of being close to the river, but clearly they were a close-knit community used defending their home against threats.

Aife now felt it extremely unlikely they would be particularly welcoming to a newcomer and was about to move on and give the place a wide berth, when she saw a small crowd of people begin to congregate in the space at the centre of the settlement. The light was beginning to fade, perhaps they too performed their ceremonies at dusk. One man passed through the crowd of onlookers, who parted as he moved through them. Judging from the reaction of the crowd, Aife guessed that this must be the leader. When he reached the middle of the crowd he gestured to two of the men standing there, who then crouched down on the floor and together lifted something away. Once they stood up again Aife could see that they were carrying a large wooden latticework frame which had clearly covered a pit of some kind. Two other men jumped down into the pit and handed up someone to the waiting arms above. The prisoner, for that was clearly what he was, was dressed raggedly and his hands were bound. Covered in mud, his hair lay over his face to the extent that Aife could not make out his features at all. As soon as he was lifted from the pit, the crowd became vocal. Aife couldn't make out what was being said but she could tell it wasn't good. Two more men grabbed the prisoner under each arm and dragged him forwards, his legs flailing out behind him. Holding aloft a burning torch, the leader of the settlement led the way into the forest, followed by the men with the prisoner and then the rest of the crowd, some of whom also carried torches, who continued to hurl abuse at the prisoner every step of the way.

Aife and Fionn headed back along the ridge the same way they had come. The noise of the crowd was loud enough that even when Aife's view of the procession was obscured by trees she could still follow their progress. After a while, the crowd of people from the settlement reached a clearing in the forest. Prominent in the clearing was a large dead tree, from which hung what looked like small offerings or gifts. As Aife got closer, she realised the offerings were actually parts of dead animals strung up on the branches.

The crowd of people formed a loose semi circle around the dead tree and at a signal from their leader, the prisoner was brought forward and the crowd fell silent. The prisoner's hands were untied and then each of his arms were bound to low hanging branches on either side of the tree. Then the leader began to speak. Aife crept a little further down the hillside, in order to hear what was being said and keeping a tight hold of the fur around Fionn's neck, as she had already caught the scent of the animal parts hanging from the tree. Though his dialect was very different from that of Aife's own people, she could still make out the gist of what the leader was saying.

"...it is once more our sad duty to deal with a demon from another realm that has wandered into our community. We cannot allow it to taint our hearts with its false promises of other worlds and peoples..."

Scarcely believing the words she was hearing, Aife worried that the unfamiliar dialect had caused her to misinterpret what was being said. Did they really believe that this poor wretch they held prisoner was some sort of being from another realm sent to harm them? Then she thought of her own experience at the archway. What was that if not the gateway to another place? She had not given much thought to whatever seemed to have followed her out of it until that moment. This settlement would not be much more than a day's journey by river from it. Perhaps the people here had good reason to fear strangers passing through.

"...therefore, we leave its fate in the hands of the forest so that we, with pure hearts, can continue to live in peace with the world around us."

The leader moved towards the prisoner and spoke a few words to him that Aife couldn't hear and then the crowd began to disperse and make its way back towards the settlement. The two men who had tied the prisoner to the dead tree, checked the ropes that bound him to the branches of the tree a final time before departing. Aife waited until they were all gone before she and Fionn crept forward. She took the pig's bladder of water from her belt and pushed aside some of the matted hair of the prisoner and put it to his lips.

"Drink this," she said, tipping the bladder so that the water spilled out over the prisoner's lips and chin. "I'm going to try and untie you."

Indistinct grunts came from the prisoner's mouth, and she tilted his head back a little, in order to make sure he was swallowing some of the water. As she did so his hair fell away from his face and Aife almost dropped the bladder full of water as she gasped in shock. Despite the blood and dirt that covered his face, Aife recognised the prisoner immediately.

It was her cousin, Cahal.

Cahal opened his eyes as Aife held back his head and blinked several times as if uncertain of what he saw.

"Aife? Is that really you? Please tell me that you're really here and that I'm not merely imagining this all."

"I'm here, " Aife replied. "Now, drink some water and then hold still whilst I try and cut you free." Cahal drank obediently and then Aife cut through the ropes binding him to the dead tree. Cahal collapsed to the ground as she did so and Aife propped him up against the tree and splashed some water on his face.

"Cahal, stay with me! Can you walk? We can't stay here..."

Cahal struggled to his feet and then, with help from Aife they began to make their way back up the hillside, with Fionn leading the way.

"It seems as if you've found a loyal friend," Cahal said, indicating Fionn. "I wouldn't have thought it possible that a wolf would be so tame."

"She's far from a pet," answered Aife, "but she seems to have decided to stay with me for now. Why are you here, Cahal?"

"I came looking for you."

"Why? You're needed on the council... there was no need to come rushing after me, I can take care of myself perfectly well."

Cahal, who had now recovered enough of his strength to walk by himself, stopped and looked at her.

"What is it?" She asked.

"Aife, you've been gone for over a year."

chapter six:
demons

"**a**fter you left things went from bad to worse," Cahal explained, once they had reached the ridge once more, gotten a fire going and Aife shared some of the food she had. "I confronted Malvyn and Bricriu in a council meeting about their plans to send Bricriu as an envoy to other settlements without the council's permission. I didn't mention it was you who gave me this information. I'd expected there to be an outcry and at first there was, with talk of asking both Malvyn and Bricriu to give up their places within the council, but little by little that dissipated and as time went on the blame was slowly shifted over to me."

"But you'd done nothing wrong..."

"It didn't matter. Malvyn began to win the council round. He can be very persuasive, after all. Then Oriana didn't want to see me anymore, which didn't come as much of a surprise and neither did her betrothal to Henwas' son, Ferghus, a few weeks later, although it certainly raised a few eyebrows around the settlement. After a month, I started to be ostracised within the council and after two months, when Bricriu began to report back about settlements that were more than willing to trade with us for our crystal, that's when I first began to hear talk that I would be asked to give up my place on it. Of course, they needed some reason other than my challenging Malvyn and Bricriu, so then suddenly I began to hear gossip that the reason Oriana had wanted nothing more to do with me is because that I was really in love with you...more than in love with you, in fact, that we were actually lovers."

"What?" spluttered Aife in disbelief, "surely nobody believed them?"

"Not at first and certainly everyone who I spoke to, told me they knew it was a lie...but little by little, I began to feel the mood of the settlement change towards me. Of course, some, like Anghus and Idelisa or Ethne, never wavered in their belief that it wasn't true, as did my parents, but they weren't enough. There were no protests when Malvyn put forward the motion for me to be removed from the council, everyone seemed to accept that it was the right thing to do."

"But that's unheard of! They can't just remove a council member... who did they get to take your place?"

"Aye, but they managed it nonetheless. No-one replaced me, Aife, it's now a council of four, with Malvyn having the deciding vote. In other words, he runs the settlement now because no-one can stand against him."

"This outrageous! He can't do this, we have to go back, we have to..."

"And do what, Aife?" said Cahal, quietly, trying to calm her down. "No-one would listen to us. Your reputation is no better than mine now, I'm sorry to say... What would you have us do when we got there? Try and seize control of the council by force?"

"Is that such a bad idea?"

"We would be killed before we got the chance. Worse, anyone who they suspected of helping us would probably be either killed or banished from the settlement. Would you want that to happen to my parents or Idelisa and her family?"

"Is that what happened to you?" Aife asked, shocked. "They banished you?"

"Not officially. It was 'suggested' that it would be best for everyone if I left, just as you had done. In the end, I agreed. I didn't want to cause my parents any more trouble or shame."

Aife put her arms around him. "I'm so sorry, Cahal. This is all my fault. If I hadn't asked Anghus to tell you, none of this..."

"You didn't do anything." said Cahal, interrupting her. "I chose to act on what you told Anghus. I could have kept quiet and everything would have been fine, that is if I would have been content to live a lie. No, I chose to speak up because I had to know the truth. Now I do. You and your father were right all along. I'm sorry I doubted you, Aife and for all the other unkind things I said."

"I would have sooner been proved wrong, than to have you suffer like you have."

"I know that and you mustn't worry, nobody blames you for what happened...nobody who matters anyway." The two of them sat in silence for a while, staring at the fire. "So, what have you been doing out here all this time? Cahal asked eventually.

Aife told him everything that had happened up until the point she'd encountered him - what had been only a week for her but over an entire year for him: about losing the skiff, how she managed to make another raft, meeting Fionn but, most importantly, about the archway and what she had seen inside it.

"But that's not possible," Cahal said once she had finished. "A place where you can move through time? How could something like that even be built and if it was why haven't we heard of this before?"

"Maybe we did and we just didn't realise it, " Aife replied, taking out her father's sword. "I saw this same symbol on the archway."

"Your sword? But Einon made it for you in the forging chamber, back home..."

"This isn't my sword, this is my father's." She told him about how she had been swapping the swords, when she'd overheard Malvyn and Bricriu, and of how Einon had previously confided in her that the metal of the sword was unlike any he'd ever seen.

"Did your father ever tell you where he'd really gotten the sword? I thought he said he'd won it in a game of chance or found it on his travels?"

"I know. It's only now that I realise he was being deliberately vague about it, but what if the real reason was that he'd stumbled across a secret that no one is supposed to know?"

"Surely he would have told someone if he had - his father or the council?"

"What if it was a secret so big and so impossible, he didn't think anyone would believe him? Or worse, that people would think he had lost his mind. It's difficult not to know this and not look at his reticence to trade with other settlements or some of the things he said, near the end of his life, when he was feverish in a new light."

"What things?"

Aife shrugged. "It's difficult to remember them all now, at the time I just thought it was another symptom of his sickness... Sometimes he seemed to think I was my mother and he would beg her forgiveness and tell her he'd tried to prepare me as best he could..."

"He could have just meant, 'preparing you for life' in general...I...well, most of the settlement, thought that he was preparing you for a place on the council, somehow..."

"That's what I thought too, but now I'm not so sure."

"If what you say is true and, as impossible as it sounds I do believe you, then we have to go back to this archway and warn people about it, even if they don't believe us at first, they'd have to believe us eventually."

"We don't need to go back to the archway, " Aife said, finally putting the thoughts that had been circulating around in her head for several days into words, "because I don't think it's the only one." She could see Cahal looked even more shocked than before. "Think about it. My father never came this far downriver; no-one from our settlement has, as far as I'm aware. There must be other archways, other portals... How else would he have found this sword?"

Cahal sat silent for a moment and then said: "This makes things even worse. What if things can come through from other places? Our whole world could be in danger..."

"I think things already did. I said I thought something had followed me out, what if I was right? What if it wasn't the first time? The people in that settlement down there, they thought you were a demon from another realm. Why would they think that, Cahal?"

"Those people have lost their minds, it's not unheard of. Settlements cut off by themselves, that distrust strangers..."

"That's not why they wanted to sacrifice you to the forest though, was it? I was there, Cahal, I heard what the leader of the settlement said when they tied you to that tree." She could see in his eyes, that he believed it too.

"I saw part of their settlement from the river. By the time I made it to the bank, there was a crowd of them waiting for me. I'd tried to tell them I meant them no harm and that I wanted to know if you'd passed by this way, instead they pulled me from my skiff and dragged me in front of their leader. He asked me all sorts of questions: Where I'd come from, where my settlement was... I told him the truth, but it didn't seem to satisfy him. In the end, his guards beat me, took all my things and threw me in the pit in the centre of the square."

"I saw them take you from the pit. That's when I decided to follow them and see what they intended to do with you."

"It's a good job you did, otherwise I wouldn't be here."

The fire was beginning to die down. "We should try and get some sleep," Aife suggested, "we've got to try and put some distance between us and this settlement tomorrow. We'll keep following the river as much as we can. We need to get to Backwater, or whatever is at the end of the river. There's something important there. I can't explain how I know that, but I just do."

"Very well," Cahal nodded.

They lay down on either side of the fire with Fionn in between them. She seemed to have accepted Cahal as another part of their strange pack, though she waited until she was sure he'd fallen asleep before she finally closed her eyes herself.

(2)

When Matthew walked out of the portal into Zone 1, the first thing he noticed was how fresh the air seemed. The playground he had known in his time had been replaced by a small wood, which sheltered the archway marking the portal's location. Matthew looked at it for a few moments, noting the spiral carving at the top of its arch. He ran his hand over its polished stone surface. It felt cool and smooth under his fingers. How many have passed by or through it over the years without realising its significance? He wondered.

The late summer evening meant there was still plenty of light left in the sky as he made his way to the edge of the wood. As he got to the tree line he could see the valley extending out in front of him. The wood let out into open meadow. There, maybe hundred yards from where he stood, a young man of about his age was busily adding more wood to a fire he had made.

Matthew's first instinct was to turn back into the wood, but it was too late - the young man had already seen him. He shouted something Matthew couldn't understand, then grabbed for the bow and arrow at his feet. Matthew put up his hands to protest, but the young man had already loosed an arrow from his bow. He felt the swish of the air being displaced next to his face as it struck the tree to his right with deadly accuracy. He looked back, shocked, towards the young man who was already loading the next arrow into his bow. The meaning was clear: that first shot had been a warning, the next would not miss him.

If I stay here, I'm dead, thought Matthew.

He turned and ran blindly back into the wood. The archway was only sixty feet away. I can just make it, he thought. He chanced a quick glance behind him and thought he could make out the shape of the young man running towards the wood through the gaps in the trees.

He's right behind me.

He felt his foot snag on something and stumbled. Suddenly, the ground was coming up to meet him. He felt a sharp pain in the side of his head and then everything went black.

[3]

It was still only just beginning to get light when they were awoken by the sounds of screaming.

"What's happening? Where's the wolf?" asked Cahal, as Fionn was nowhere to be seen.

"She must have gone hunting, she'll be back at some point," Aife replied, looking over the ridge. "It's coming from the settlement, something's going on down there." She could see fires burning in the main square and people running to and fro. Perhaps a fire had started in one of the buildings and they were trying to put it out. Then she saw them: several large black shapes moving around amongst the smoke. They walked like men, but looked bigger and bulkier and they carried something in their hands. Something that shot out fire and light. As Aife stood watching, she saw the black shapes turn two men, who were running for cover, into balls of flame. The men collapsed on the ground, screaming for a few moments, and then were still. "I'm going down there, " she said.

"Don't, Aife, you'll be killed. Those people are savages - who knows how many strangers they've sacrificed to the forest over the years?"

"I can't stand by and watch an entire settlement slaughtered like animals. No matter what they've done, they don't deserve this. Now, will you help me or not?"

They made their way down the hillside as quickly and quietly as they could.

"What's the plan?," asked Cahal, as they crouched by some trees on the edge of the settlement. "We don't have any weapons other than your sword..."

Aife looked towards the main square. A small boy, maybe 5 or 6 years of age was there by the animal pens. He was holding a young lamb and crying, whilst struggling to open the gate of the pen. One of the black shapes had spotted him and was advancing towards the child. "Then we'll have to get some more..." she said, before rushing out from the trees with her sword, towards the black shape and the boy.

As she ran, the words of Aife's fighting teacher echoed in her head. She had been a lot smaller than most of the boys she'd had to train alongside. He teacher had taught her to use that to her advantage.

The bigger the opponent, the longer their reach, he had taught her. *Don't let them grab hold of you. You are smaller and faster than they are. Strike hard at their legs, use their extra weight to knock them off balance and then, once they are on the ground, attack quickly to immobilise them.*

Aife swung her sword at the legs of the black shape with all the force she could muster. The leg came clean away and the shape toppled backwards onto the ground.

Now she was closer she could see the shape was made from a shiny black metal that covered its entire body, like a kind of armour. It was at least as big as Anghus, if not taller still. Its face, whilst shaped like that of a person's, had no features save a narrow slit that bisected its entire visage from forehead to chin and glowed faintly with a blueish white light from underneath. The rest of its face was smooth and polished just like its body. With a downward stroke of her sword, she decapitated it. The shape's headless corpse shuddered for a few seconds before becoming still. Aife wrenched the weapon from its lifeless fingers and tossed it to Cahal, who had come running over to where she stood.

"What am I supposed to do with this?," he asked, weighing the unfamiliar weapon in his hands.

"It shoots out fire, there must be some mechanism on it that makes it work." She unlocked the pen, freeing

111

the little boy and the lamb and then letting out the rest of the animals from their pens too. "Look for a lever or something and press it while pointing the thing!"

Cahal moved the weapon around in his hands for a few moments, searching its underside. "Aha!" he said, finding the trigger at last and then gasped as a bright light shot out from the end of the weapon and hit a tree, fifteen feet away, which immediately burst into flames. "What is this thing?"

"Never mind what it is, just use it!" shouted Aife and pointed towards two more black shapes coming at them out of the smoke. Cahal turned and fired at them, knocking one of them down, whilst Aife struck out at the other with her sword.

Despite their size and bulk the shapes were surprisingly fast and agile and attacking one "head on" proved far more difficult. As Aife tried to swipe at the arm holding the weapon with her sword, the shape back handed her with its other arm with enough force to send her hurtling several feet away. She landed on her back with a grunt.

The smoke from the burning houses was now so thick it was impossible to see more than a few steps in front of you. Plus, the smoke stung her eyes and throat making her cough. She shouted for Cahal, but there was no reply. He probably couldn't hear her over the noise of the screaming and the incessant crackle of the flames. She could hear people and animals running around nearby even though she couldn't see them because of the smoke. A pig brushed against her leg as it hurried past, squealing in terror, and then someone collided with her, knocking Aife to the ground once more and the sword from her hand.

Panicking, she searched blindly on her hands and knees for it. Her eyes were streaming now and she was forced to blink constantly in order to be able to see anything out of them at all. At last, she felt the familiar hilt of her father's sword under her fingers and pulled it towards her with great relief. As she did so, she felt a hand grab her by the hair and yank her off her knees, dragging her along the ground. She tried to strike out at the hand that held her with the sword, but her assailant caught her by the wrist and then dragged her by that too. Then, her attacker pulled inside one of the buildings and threw her to the ground.

Sheltered from the smoke now, Aife found she could see a little better once more. Blinking, she tried to struggle to her feet and came face to face with her attacker. He was clearly a man, but not like any she'd ever encountered before. He wore similar armour to that of the black shapes. A large scar ran down the side of his face, which was deathly pale, and his mouth was covered in some sort of mask. When he spoke his voice sounded metallic and grating.

"Your sword," he growled, grabbing hold of her arm tightly. "Where did you find it?" .

"I didn't find it, it belongs to me!"

The pale man's eyes narrowed. "Don't lie to me!" he rasped. "This sword was stolen from me a long time ago by a young boy about your age. He would be old now. Where is he?"

"He's dead...he was my father..."

From behind his mask the pale man's expression softened. He loosened his grip on Aife's wrist and no longer looked angry . "You don't come from here, where is your 'settlement'?" The way he said 'settlement' seemed to suggest he was unsure if it was the right word to use. "Tell me! I need to find it, it's important.."

Aife opened her mouth to speak but no words came out. Then, out of the corner of her eye, she caught a glimpse of a bright flash of light and felt a sudden warmth brush past her. She collapsed to the floor and when she looked up, she saw the pale man lying a few feet away from her, his armour smouldering.

"Aife! Are you alright?" Cahal helped her to feet and she lent against him for a few moments as she continued to get her breath back. "Can you walk? We need to get out of here. The whole settlement is ablaze. Those that are left are heading for the river and whatever craft they can find, we should go too." Aife nodded. Cahal tore a strip of fabric from his clothes and tied it over Aife's nose and mouth. She saw that he had done the same. "This will help a little with the smoke," he said. Her gaze shifted over to the pale man once more. He lay on the ground as before, not stirring. The walls and floor were beginning to burn around him as sparks from the fires outside drifted in on the wind, and caught hold on any loose bits of straw. "He's dead, forget about him," Cahal said.

"I don't think so. We need to take him with us."

"Have you lost your mind? He tried to kill you..."

"No, he wanted to know about my father and our settlement. He said that my father had stolen the sword from him. Somehow, he's the key to all of this. If we really want to protect ourselves and our world, then we have to know what we're up against. If we leave him to die here, we'll have no more answers than we did before. Besides, even if he does look like a monster, I still can't leave him to burn to death."

Struggling with the pale man's weight, the two of them dragged him as best they could from the burning building. Aife chopped away a piece of the wooden fence that had surrounded the animal pens and then they lay the pale man on top of it and pulled his body along on it like a makeshift sledge. The smoke was so thick that they shifted direction more than once as Cahal tried get his bearings and find out which direction the river was, but at last they came to a clearing in the trees and could make out the water ahead of them.

The way to the river lead them along a wooden walkway to sort of jetty, where they could see members of the settlement frantically scrambling into any waterborne vessel that would carry them. Some had lashed several skiffs together, allowing them and their families and some of their animals to all come aboard.

"You!" Aife heard the scream mixed with a shout from behind her as the leader of the settlement leapt at Cahal. The force of his attack knocked them both over and Aife and Cahal were forced to let go of the body of the pale man as they were sent sprawling across the wooden walkway. Aife looked up to see Cahal doing his best to fight off the leader, who was brandishing a small axe made of flint.

"You brought the demons who destroyed our home, I should have cut your throat the moment I saw you!" the leader shouted at him. He buried the axe in Cahal's shoulder and Cahal screamed in pain as blood gushed from the wound.

"Cahal!" Aife cried out, as she got to her feet and rushed towards the pair with her sword drawn.

"Go, Aife!" Cahal shouted to her and then summoning all his strength, grabbed the leader and pulled them both off the walkway and down into the water below.

"No!" she screamed and ran along the walkway, jumped down on to the jetty and from there into the water, where the two were still struggling. She was too late, however, and got there just as the leader, who had managed to get on top of Cahal in the water, rained down a series of furious axe blows on top of her cousin's head. The water turned red with blood and she saw

Cahal's grip on the leader's arm loosen and his hand fall away, slack, into the water.

Enraged, Aife charged at the leader with her sword drawn but was grabbed by several other men from the settlement, who held her firmly.

"You are also a demon sent here to destroy us, so you shall meet the same fate as your companion!" the leader said, as he approached Aife with the blood-spattered axe in his hand. He turned and addressed the remaining members of the settlement on the jetty or in the water readying their craft: "Death to the demons who walk among us!" He shouted and raised the axe above his head.

A burst of light hit the man holding Aife's right arm, and the force of the blast knocked them both backwards into the water. Aife felt it sear her right side. Spluttering from the water she had just swallowed, Aife stood up again only to see the man to her left hit in the chest by a blast of light as well, and fall back into the water, his flaming wound making a hissing sound as he went under. She looked up to see the pale man, holding the weapon Cahal had been carrying, jump down into the water next to her and face off against the leader.

"Morfran!", The leader shouted, "You have no right to enter our realm, return to the darkness from whence you came!" and with that he rushed at the pale man, swinging his axe. There was a blast of light from the pale man's weapon and the leader fell back into the water in a fountain of steam. The pale man grabbed Aife by the shoulder and pulled her towards him.

"Are you hurt?" he asked as he held her close. "Stay with me, I'll get us out of this..."   There was a snarl from behind them and then Aife was knocked into the water once more. When she surfaced she saw Fionn attacking the pale man, who was using his armour-covered arms to protect his face from her snapping jaws. Aife swam over to where she thought the pale man might have dropped his weapon. After a few seconds of searching she felt it under her hands.

"Here, Fionn!", she shouted and the wolf left the pale man and came to her side. She aimed the weapon at the water beside him, which exploded in a cloud of steam, then she pointed the weapon directly at his chest.

"One step closer and I'll kill you!", she shouted at the pale man.

"I'm not your enemy", he replied. "I've been looking for the person who has that sword for many years. You've seen the archways, I'm guessing you know what they do?..." Aife nodded.

"They move you through time."

"That's right... and I come from that other time. One that needs your help..."

"Why should I help you? You and those things came here and killed all these people."

"I came here looking for you, or whomever had the sword. These people attacked me just as they did you, just now. Those "things" as you call them, were here to protect me." he pointed to his scarred face. "I got this on my first visit here, from your father... This time I came prepared." The pale man stepped towards her. Fionn growled. Aife raised the weapon slightly and winced at the pain in her side as she did so. "You are hurt", he said, noticing the wound. "Please let me take a look at it..."

"Stay back!", Aife shouted. The weapon suddenly felt heavy in her hands, however. She felt her knees buckle and then cold water hit her face before she blacked out

chapter seven:
safe

[1]

matthew felt the hands on his face. He tried to open his eyes, but the right hand side of his face felt tight and swollen and found that his right lid wouldn't open. He instinctively put his hands to his face and realised that there was some sort of dressing on that side of his head.

"Try not to touch it," said a kindly voice nearby.

Matthew turned his head slightly and with his left eye was able to see the young woman kneeling next to him. Her age was hard to guess, though she looked a little older than he was. She was dressed in white and her jet black hair was long and braided. She reached out and took his hand in her own.

"It's alright," she said, "you're safe, now."

"Where am I?"

"In my home, I found you in the forest - you were badly hurt. I brought you back here and looked after you. You were asleep for some time..."

"Thank you, I..." Matthew stopped in mid-sentence, suddenly realising the incongruity of what was happening. "You can understand me, how is that possible?"

The woman smiled. "Because we share a secret. One that few others are even aware of..."

Matthew stared at her. From underneath her tunic she brought forth the pendant that hung around her neck. Matthew immediately recognised the spiral symbol that was carved into it.

"My bag," he said suddenly. "I had a bag that I was carrying with me..."

"Here," she said, handing him the rucksack.

He emptied everything in it but there was no sign of the sword.

"Where's my sword?"

"This was everything I found, lying beside you," the woman replied. "I repacked everything back into the bag."

"Back into the bag? Was it open then?"

"Yes...there was another man...he was there when I arrived. He ran off. He was going through your things...He had a sword..."

Matthew groaned.

"Does it matter?"

"Yes! The sword...it had this same symbol on it," he said, pointing to her pendant. "It was my key to the portal - without it I'm stuck here!"

"I have two keys," she replied. "How else would I have been able to bring you here?"

"Here?"

Matthew got up and stood swaying for a few seconds, before lurching towards the entrance of the woman's house.

"Take it easy, you're not well enough yet to go running around!" She tried to get him to lie back down but Matthew was having none of it.

Outside, the sunlight was dazzling and he had to shield his good eye from its glare. All around him were huts of various sizes, scattered around the banks of a small stream, interspersed with areas reserved for livestock and arable land. On the far side of the stream, the land rose up steadily towards rocky hills that sheltered the settlement and its inhabitants from strong winds and attack from the north.

Something about the shape of the terrain seemed familiar to him. Looking around again, as several of the members of the settlement broke off from what they were doing to stare at the stranger in their midst, it suddenly came to him:

He was home.

It was the shape of the hills that convinced him, though in his time they had been flattened to a certain extent by many centuries of building, they were the same hills that he looked on from the balcony of the penthouse flat.

"This is Zone 5," he said to the woman, who was now leading him slowly back to her hut. "This is where I live..."

She made him lie back down where he'd been before and gently removed the dressing on the right hand side of his face. Matthew suddenly pushed her away from him and grabbed for the first aid kit, inside his rucksack. In the kit was a small mirror. He held it up to his face to inspect the damage but dropped it as soon as he caught sight of his reflection.

His face was bruised and swollen and he had a deep cut that extended from next to his eyebrow all the way down the right side of his face, ending just above the corner of his mouth.

"It's me," he gasped. "I'm Morfran."

"Pleased to meet you, Morfran," said the woman. "My name is Medb."

[2]

When Aife awoke she found herself looking up at a ceiling in a dwelling not much different from her uncle's. Like Matthew, she found the woman dressed completely in white sat beside her. She smiled when she saw Aife looking over at her.

"Don't be afraid, my child. You are completely safe here."

"Where am I?" Aife asked, trying to sit up.

"Take it easy, lie back down again" said the woman's soothing voice, "you were badly hurt and whilst the wound is better, you still need to rest." The mention of the wound set Aife's mind racing once more and, as if anticipating the question that was forming in her mind, the woman said: "Your wolf is right here, she is perfectly fine. She has not left your side the whole time."

Aife turned her head and saw that Fionn lay curled up near her feet. The wolf yawned and gave a soft whine when she saw Aife look across at her.

"It is quite remarkable that she is so fond of you," the woman said as she held out a hand to Fionn, who sniffed it tentatively and then licked it. "You must have shown her great kindness to win her trust so completely."

"How did I get here?"

"You were brought here. This is my home and I have been looking after you, these past few days."

"But the man with the scar...they said his name was 'Morfran'..."

"He was the one who brought you here."

"But.."

Once again, Aife tried to sit up. This time, the woman put her hand on Aife's chest and gently pushed her back down on to the bed and gave her some water to drink.

"I know you must have many questions. I will try to give you some of the answers you seek, but only if you promise to rest, understand?" Aife nodded. "That's better" said the woman. "Tell me, what is your name?"

"Aife."

"A good strong name...a warrior's name. I am Medb. This Morfran - that is not his real name. It is the name

125

he chose to call himself in this time. It means "an ugly demon."

The words of the leader of the settlement upriver came back to Aife as Medb said this. "When I first met him he was just a young man. Since then he has returned many times. He has been searching for something here, always asking the same questions: about the sword, the young man who took it and where he might come from."

"He means my father..."

"So I understand," Medb replied.

"What does he want with my settlement?"

"Perhaps it's better that he answers that himself, once you are better."

"Is he here?"

Medb shook her head. "No, he has returned to his own time." Sensing Aife's unease, she added: "Despite his appearance, he is nothing to be afraid of. I was the one who nursed him back to health when he got that scar."

There was a knock from outside and a young man about the same age as Aife came in carrying some food. His hair was the colour of fresh straw and his face seemed kind.

"Aife, I'd like you to meet Annan", Medb said as he put the food down next to Aife. "He's my son."

"Pleased to meet you" Annan said. "Mother thought you might be hungry, so I brought you both some food. I also brought a bone for the wolf..."

"Her name's Fionn. Here, give me the bone and I'll give it to her. She's not a pet and I don't want her to bite you."

"She won't bite me, don't worry. I've fed her the last two days, so I think she sees me as a friend, now." He held out the bone to Fionn, who took it extremely politely from Annan's open hand.

"She's clearly taken to you," Aife said, as Fionn took the bone back to her place at the foot of her bedding and began gnawing on it with relish.

"Annan has something of a gift with animals, much like you" said Medb, smiling, as Aife began tucking into the food she had been brought.

Once they had all finished eating, Annan excused himself once more, saying he still had some chores to attend to.

Once he had gone, Medb changed the dressing on Aife's wound. "Yes, that's healing up nicely," she said. "A few more days and you'll be as good as new."

When she was dressed once more, Aife brought out her father's sword. "Is there a stone archway near here with this symbol on it?"

Medb nodded. "There is one not far from here. That is my role in this settlement: to take my knowledge of the archways and use it to guide the settlement as best I can." She produced the talisman with the same symbol from under her tunic.

"Guide them how?"

"You've been through one, you know how it works..."

"It allows you to travel through time."

"Exactly. I can use it to discover threats to our settlement before they happen and then alter the path, so they don't come about."

"So you change the future. Isn't that dangerous?"

"I only change small things. The ones given this knowledge have to make difficult choices because only we know what might have been."

"Doesn't the rest of the settlement know about them?"

"Without a key, it is merely an archway. Only those that have a key, like the one in your sword, can pass through the archway and reach the portal," she said, confirming what Aife had already suspected. "The people here have long accepted it as a shrine or special place. They know it has power, they just don't know what that power really is. Only one person in the settlement has that knowledge, the rest of the settlement does not worry about something it doesn't know."

"What about those that come here from other times, doesn't that raise questions?"

"It might surprise you to know that there have been remarkably few. The more people that know the truth about the archways, the more the danger of them being used for the wrong purpose increases."

"How many archways are there?"

"Five."

"How do you know?"

"Because the portals told me so. Did you not realise that all the portals are connected, that you can move between one or another instantly?" Aife thought back to the coloured lights on the panel, each with their own symbol - so that had been their meaning.

"Have you visited each of them?"

"Yes, though I have never spent much time at the other locations, as I didn't want to draw attention to myself. Is there one near your settlement?"

"Not that I know of. No one in my settlement had ever talked about one... or at least that's what I thought."

"That doesn't mean there wasn't one nearby, merely that no one knew its real purpose. These archways have stood for a thousand generations or more, but most people think they are just part of an old ruin. Tell me about the one you entered."

"It was in a clearing in the forest, several days journey downriver from my settlement... I saw it glinting through the trees."

"That would be Zone 4. I happen to know that your father encountered Morfran near Zone 1 - high up in the hills where the river begins."

"That would make sense. I know he travelled far into the hills above our settlement as a young man and it was on one of these journeys that he came back with the sword. He told no one about Morfran or the archways, not even when he was dying."

"You resent him for not telling you?"

"Of course! I thought I knew my father - now I've found out he kept a secret from me all my life."

"Perhaps he wanted to spare you the burden of what that knowledge might bring. To keep a secret to oneself, when you know it can only harm others, is actually a brave thing to do, Aife..."

"It seems to me that he was just scared and that eventually the knowledge ate away at him until it consumed him."

"Bravery and fear are not opposites, Aife. They are part of the same circle. Fear can cause acts of incredible bravery, just as bravery often masks a secret fear. Knowledge of the archways is a huge responsibility and often it brings misery. Maybe you shouldn't see your father not telling you about them as something bad, but as an example of how much he loved you. He wanted to spare from it until you were ready."

Aife thought about this for a moment. Seen in this light, all of the things her father had made her learn, despite the objections of the council and others in the settlement, made complete sense. They hadn't been to prepare her to take his seat on the council at all. They had been to prepare for the day her world might be turned upside down. Even asking Einon to make Aife a copy of his sword, now made her question whether or not its real purpose hadn't been for him to discover just how unusual the sword was. It also made her think more kindly of her father's reticence in expanding the trade of their crystal with settlements beyond the outliers, because it would have undoubtably drawn more attention to the settlement and perhaps Morfran would have been more likely to find him and the sword because of that.

Medb saw her thinking all of this and smiled once more.

"I think that's enough questions for now. There will be plenty more time to talk, later on but, for now, you should rest a little more."

Aife did as she was told and lay back on the bedding again. Her eyelids felt heavy. She closed them and fell asleep almost immediately.

(3)

Matthew thought long and hard about his future plans in the days that followed. He told Medb about the lepidolite, but she had no idea where it might be mined other than that it couldn't be anywhere near by, or she would have heard about it. She also had no idea who the young man with the bow and arrow had been. He had run off just as she arrived and she'd never seen him before. He began to make a mental list of what he would need if he had any hope of continuing the search for the lepidolite mine.

He realised in retrospect that he should have been more prepared. He had no hope of learning whatever Celtic or Brythonic language was spoken in this time, yet he needed a way to communicate with the people he met here.

He also needed a way to protect himself. It had been naive of him to think that any of his modern day skills would be a match for a culture where everyone could wield a sword, bow or axe better than he ever could - and he had the scar to prove it! Despite using the cauterising suture in his first aid kit to seal up the wound, its mark would be there for the rest of his life, just as it was on his future self.

At Medb's insistence he'd mostly confined himself to her home, except for when the two of them had gone for walks together around her settlement. He enjoyed her company and she seemed to enjoy his, though their talks mostly consisted of him asking her lots of questions about this time: How long the settlement had been here, her role in it - which seemed to involve her using the portals to help the settlement without changing anything so drastically that they would effect the future dramatically - and how much she knew about the portals. She answered his questions as best she could, though he always thought she was holding something back. If she had questions about him and the time he had come from, she kept them to herself.

"Aren't you curious about the time where I come from?"

"It's better for me not to be."

"Surely it's just normal though - to want to know what the future would be like?"

"Yes...and obviously, the temptation is there, but I don't want to give into it." She turned suddenly as she said this and kissed him, briefly, on the cheek. "If you're wise, you'll stay in your own time once you return - it's not good to dwell on the past, or the future."

"You know I can't do that," Matthew replied, taking her hand in his. "My world is dying. I have to do something to stop that."

"How do you know that it won't die anyway, no matter what you do?"

"I don't, but knowing that I could do something to help means I have to try. You must understand that?"

She touched his face. "You're a good man, but you're still only a man. You've already come close to dying in your travels through the portals, how much more are you prepared to risk?"

"Everything, if that's what's needed."

"That's noble..." she said and lent forward and kissed him again, this time on the mouth, "...but also foolish." Her lips felt warm despite the cold morning air.

Matthew just stood there, open mouthed. She giggled at his expression.

"Was it really that bad?" She asked as she leant in and kissed him again, more slowly this time.

"No, not at all," Matthew replied and realised he was blushing. He took her in his arms and kissed her properly this time.

"You could just stay here with me," she said softly, as their lips parted once more.

"I know," he replied, leaning over slightly so that their foreheads touched. "And I also know I'd be happy staying here, with you, which is why it makes it doubly hard not to - but that's what I have to do. I'll leave tomorrow."

She nodded as he put his arms around her.

(4)

The days passed and Aife's wound healed. Eventually, Medb pronounced her well enough to go outside a little. This gave Aife her first proper view of the settlement where Medb and Annan lived. The river came in through a narrow tunnel in a rocky cliff. Once through the tunnel, the water then opened out into a sort of large pool around which the settlement was built, mostly made up of crannog buildings jutting out over the water, before trickling off into a small stream that ran out into the fields beyond. This was where the river, such as she had known it, ended. This was 'Backwater'. Morfran had somehow managed to bring both her and Fionn here on a raft after she'd lost consciousness.

As the days passed, Annan showed Aife and Fionn around the settlement a little. A large group of children often came with them, curious about the stranger in their midst and even more so about her four-legged friend. None of them had ever seen a wolf in the flesh before and they all wanted to see Fionn up close and stroke her soft fur. Aife was a little unsure of how Fionn might react to all this attention and at first had to remind the children that the wolf was not a pet or an animal used to being handled by humans. She needn't have worried though. Fionn took this new found popularity in her stride and happily let the various children make a fuss of her.

She grew to like Annan a lot. He was a good listener and seemed genuinely interested in hearing about her life and what she had seen on her journey downriver. The majority of his settlement never travelled beyond the high rocky cliff, that separated them from the world beyond it and even he had only travelled beyond its boundaries via the archway. The cliff created a natural barrier between the settlement and the other side. Aife imagined that, from a distance, most travellers heading downstream would believe that the river simply flowed underground from that point onwards. From the settlement side, the cliff to the left of the pool went up more or less vertically, whereas on the right-hand side it sloped gradually, allowing for spaces where crops could be grown or animals could graze, which could be accessed by one of the many small wooden bridges than ran across the stream. She and Annan spent many hours walking in this part of the settlement, though often Aife's thoughts were preoccupied with the thought that eventually she would need to meet with Morfran once more.

Though she had asked Medb lots of questions about him, she only received some of the answers she sought. Medb seemed extremely fond of him and he had clearly saved Aife's life, both back at the other settlement and by bringing her here, but that did little to change her unease towards him and that unease was compounded one day when Medb revealed that he was Annan's father.

"So you and him were together?"

"Briefly, but it's not as straight forward as that - I am not Annan's birth mother."

"But you call him your son?"

"And to all intents and purposes I am his mother - I have raised him since he was just a baby - but he was born in Morfran's time and brought back to this one."

"Why?"

"To keep him safe."

"Is the future dangerous?"

"No more than any other time. However, something happened in Morfran's time to put Annan's life in jeopardy."

"Because he's Morfran's son?"

"It seems so. He came to me one night with Annan, when he was just a baby. Morfran had blood on his clothes. He begged me to look after his son and raise him as my own. He said unless he could change what happens to his world, Annan would not be safe. "

"He told me his world needs my help."

"It does."

"But you still won't tell me how I'm supposed to help him?"

"No. It's better that he does that himself - once you are better." Seeing her unease, Medb repeated her assurance that Aife had no need to be afraid of Morfran.

Try as she might, however, she couldn't block out the memory of the black shapes and the burning settlement and the fear in that little boy's eyes...

"It bothers you, doesn't it? That Morfran's my father."

Annan had been showing her around the settlement once again and, as usual Aife's mind had been elsewhere.

"Medb told you she'd told me?"

Annan nodded. "She knows you're worried about seeing him again - but there's no need to be. He's not someone to be afraid of."

"Tell that to the settlement he burnt to the ground, further up river," Aife replied, rather more bitterly than she'd meant to.

Annan was silent for a moment. "I'm sorry," she said, eventually. "That was mean... I know he saved my life and I know he's your father, but you didn't see what he did..."

"Did your father ever do anything you didn't agree with?"

"He never killed anyone..."

"...that you know of." They stopped walking and Annan turned and looked at her. "I won't make excuses for what he's done, but he is desperate for your help.

Desperate people sometimes do terrible things in the name of necessity."

"But the weapons he has and those black shapes - nobody in our time stands a chance against them...."

"You can't really begrudge him for coming with an army after what happened with your father and that isn't the only occasion when he's been attacked, in this time or in others."

"Do you know what happened between them?"

"All I know that your father left him for dead and that Medb saved his life."

"That doesn't sound like my father - there must be more to it than that."

"Maybe, but it might also be that you didn't know your father as well as you thought."

"I feel as though I barely knew him at all these days," she replied, sadly.

They were standing in the section closest to where the land rose up into the cliff. There was a part that was separated from the rest. No animals grazed there and there seemed to be no crops either. Instead it was full of wild flowers and the ground was occasionally broken up by what looked like small markers made of wood.

"What's that area?" Aife asked, looking for a way to change the subject.

Annan looked at her slightly surprised. "It's the place where we bury the bodies of the dead."

Now it was Aife's turn to be surprised. "You bury them? In the ground?"

"Yes, of course. Doesn't your settlement do that?"

"No, I've heard that some of the outliers bury their dead together in large burial places, but our settlement has never done that. We pack the bodies into a skiff and send them off downriver to..." She stopped herself before she said it, as her thoughts suddenly caught up with her.

"This is where they end up. Along with those who die here." He stopped and looked at Aife. Sensing her silence, he said: "I'm sorry, it wasn't my intention to upset you...we don't feel any animosity towards those that send their dead to us - we see it as part of our communal duty to look after the remains of those who arrive here. Surely you must have realised that eventually the bodies would wash up somewhere and have to be dealt with?"

"To tell you the truth, I don't think I ever really gave it much thought...I don't think anyone in my settlement did. The river was the one constant in our lives and we had no idea how far it went. No-one, to my knowledge, has ever made a journey downstream as far as this. For all we knew it might have gone on forever, for us the river is the pathway to the world of the ancestors. Is it not the same here? "

"No, here there would be no point in consigning the dead to water that flows back into the ground. Instead, like the water, we return the bodies of the dead to the earth, so that as their bodies decay their nutrients feed the land and the plants. Does that make sense?"

Aife had to admit that it did. She looked at the small wooden markers by the different graves. "These mark each of the bodies?," she asked. Annan nodded. "Is there any way to tell which body is which?" she said.

"Medb marks each with the date when they were buried, and the name of the person if it is someone from the settlement." he said pointing to the markings.

Aife ran her fingers over the lines that had been cut into it. "I saw the same symbols inside the archway, but I didn't know what they meant."

"Yes, they're called numbers..." Annan said.

"Numbers?"

"Yes, symbols for how many things you have of something: one, two, three... "

"Oh, we just use lines: one line, two lines...why do you need symbols?"

"So we don't have to count up the lines," Annan replied. "Suppose you need to write down really big amounts of things, like how many trees were in a forest?"

"Well we have a system for counting in groups of twenty, but why would anyone need to count all the trees in a forest?" Aife asked laughing.

"Ok forget the trees, how would count how many days there were in a year?

"Well... I guess you'd have to make a line for each day, and then once you got to twenty you'd convert it into one of those. If you started at the beginning of summer, then by the beginning of next summer you'd know...but of course it would be difficult know for certain you started and ended on the same day..."

Annan nodded. "Some years, summer starts earlier, sometimes winter is early. What if there was a way to measure the time exactly?"

"How is that possible?"

"By using symbols for numbers. It's essential in order to travel through time. How else would you know how far you were going, if you couldn't describe large units of time accurately? How could you do that if you couldn't know exactly how many days there are in a year or if you couldn't divide the days up into parts, so that you could know exactly at what point in the day you were?"

"They divide the day into parts?" He had awoken her curiosity now. She still couldn't grasp how the symbols were able to do all this, but she instinctively grasped how important this was to using the archways and if that was the case she needed to understand it as much as possible.

"Into twenty-four equal parts, twelve for the daytime and twelve for the night."

"But how were they able to do that? I mean...during the day I understand, you could look at the height of the sun and see the time changing and I suppose if you were to take the time, then you could measure how long it took to move but how did they know it was exactly right? And what about in the winter when the day seems shorter and the nights longer, how were they able to measure it then?

Annan shook his head. "I have no idea. All I know is, that's what they did. Then they divided each of those twelve parts into another sixty equal parts, so that not only do you know what part of the day you're going to but at what exact moment. They also divide the year into twelve parts too, but there they don't do it equally, for some reason, because some parts of the year have more days than others."

"That doesn't make any sense."

"I know it doesn't. Maybe they just liked the idea of dividing it by twelve again..."

"I still don't understand how the symbols work, can you explain them to me? They should tell me the exact day that this person was buried here, is that correct?"

"Yes, that's right. Starting from this end: these two symbols tell you the day, these two symbols tell you which of the twelve parts of the year and these last six tell you the year..."

"How did they know which year was the first one?"

"I don't know. All I know is that my mother based these numbers on those within the archway, which always tells you exactly what moment you're currently in - otherwise, again, how would you know how far you were going or when you needed to get back to?"

"Yes, of course. Can you read the numbers?"

"Yes. It's actually a very simple system. Each amount from one to nine has its own individual symbol, there's also a symbol for nothing."

"Why do you need a symbol for nothing?"

"I'm just coming to that. So the symbol for nothing is this circle," Annan replied, pointing to one of the markers. "Once you get to ten, then they use two symbols: the symbol for one and the symbol for nothing and then the symbols start repeating: eleven is the symbol for one and another symbol for one, twelve is the symbol for one and the symbol for two and so on until you get to twenty, then the first of the two symbols changes to the symbol for two and the pattern begins again. That goes on through until the two symbols reach the symbol for a nine and another nine and then it becomes three symbols and the pattern begins again. In a way it's quite clever, because it means you only have to learn ten individual symbols and then you can write large amounts of things easily."

"Alright, teach me the other individual symbols up to nine."

"Sure," Annan replied. He scanned the markers for the respective numbers. "So this is the symbol for one - that's easy, it's just like a line. Here's two:" he said, pointing at the symbol she had thought had resembled a river. Aife couldn't stop herself from giggling at the memory of what she had thought the symbol for three resembled and neither could Annan once she'd told him what was so funny. When he had gone through the symbols, she practiced by reading out the days and parts of the year from the various grave markers that Annan chose for her at random.

"Can we see if we can find where my father's body is buried? It would have been about a year ago, if he's here."

"Of course," Annan replied and guided Aife through the stones to some further back. "These would have been from last year. We can ignore any with names, they would have been people from the settlement. For those that we don't know, we often remove one of the offerings included with them and place them by the grave marker." Armed with this knowledge it was easy to identify the burial place belonging to Aife's father - a familiar looking sword was planted into the ground next to the plot. "I'll leave you to your thoughts," Annan said as they stood in front of the burial plot. "I'll be just over there when you're ready."

Aife reached out for his hand and held it, stopping him from going. "Stay," she said, and the two of them stood there in front of her father's grave in silence, holding hands.

"I'm sorry about your father," Annan said at last, "but you really don't need to be afraid of mine, you'll see. I'll even come with you when you go to see him, if you want?"

"Really?" Aife turned to look at Annan but didn't let of his hand. Aife felt suddenly overcome by the desire not to break that closeness until she had to and she noticed that Annan showed the same reluctance.

"Sure." He smiled. Aife liked it when he smiled. The moment was broken by Medb's voice as she approached. Fionn was with her.

"There you are! I wondered where you'd got to, but I suppose I should have guessed that you would come here, eventually. I see you have found your father's resting place, Aife."

"Yes," she said, "and Annan has been teaching me the number system that the archways use."

"Very good," Medb replied. "Let's put your new found knowledge to the test."

[5]

The first rays of the dawn had just begun to peak over the hill surrounding the settlement when Medb and Matthew made their way towards the small forest where the portal was. Neither of them spoke on the way. There was nothing to be said. When they reached the archway, she gripped his hand tightly, holding him back. He twisted around in her grip and reached up to touch her cheek with his free hand. She kissed his hand and pulled him close to her and kissed him on the lips.

"I'll miss you," he said.

"You know where to find me, when you do..."

"I know 'when' to find you," he replied. "I'm not going anywhere, except in time."

145

"That's what makes it harder," she said trying to smile, "knowing that we'll only be metres apart, but divided by thousands of years." She handed him her spare talisman. "Don't lose this one."

"I won't, I'll guard it with my life."

"I should hope so."

"How can I ever thank you?"

"By looking after yourself...don't risk so much that there's nothing left."

Medb embraced him one more time and then stood back to let him go. With a final wave, Matthew turned and walked through the archway. In a second he was gone.

"You know he'll fail - he has to..." said a voice from behind Medb.

"Maybe," she replied, not turning around to face the man in white as he stepped out from behind one of the trees, "maybe you underestimate just how determined he is..."

"Blind hope and determination won't be enough," said the man in white who was now standing beside Medb, "they never are..."

"How would you know Kynthelig?" she asked, turning on him. "How would any of us know what it must feel like to carry that sort of burden?"

"You could have just let him die. You should have, instead of pulling the knot this man has created even tighter."

"You do a good job of sounding like you don't care, when I know full well that's not the case."

"At least I wouldn't have fallen in love with him. Well I hope he was worth it...give me your key, you know the rules."

She took the talisman from around her neck and put it in his hand. "I'd do it again without a second thought."

part two:
the journey back

Tomorrow is nothing, today is too late; the good lived yesterday.

Marcus Aurelius

chapter eight:
moments in time

ife, Annan, Medb and Fionn made their way through the settlement, following the stream until they came to the small forest where the archway stood. No bracken or moss grew around this one, however, Aife noticed. This one bore clear signs of careful tending. Someone had obviously taken great care, for example, in weeding the grass around it so that it stood there, clear and proud as if it had only just arrived.

If Medb was surprised at Annan's suggestion that he should accompany Aife, she didn't show it. She sat down on a stone near the archway, with Fionn at her feet.

"We'll be waiting for you here" she said.

Annan had his own talisman, much like Medb's, and as the two of them went through the archway the lights of the controls flickered on and Aife was entranced by their beauty, once more.

"How do they make them glow so beautifully?" she asked Annan.

"It's a form of artificial light, made without the use of fire and heat." He stepped forward to the control panel and beckoned Aife to come closer as well. "This is how the archways measure time," he said, pointing at the sequence of numbers at the top of the control panel. "These numbers constantly change to show you the exact moment you are currently in, starting from this end they show you: the day, the part of the year and the year itself, followed by the division of the day or night into twenty-four equal parts, and then a division of that into sixty and then into sixty again."

"Their precision in dividing time into smaller and smaller units is staggering. It hurts me to even think how long it must have taken them to arrive at these amounts."

"Do you remember what I told you about the uneven division of the parts of the year?"

"The twelve parts aren't all the same. Some parts have more days than others."

"That's right. In some thirty-one, in others thirty and, most bizarrely, in the second part of the year, twenty-eight, except for every four years where there are twenty-nine."

"But why would they use such a flawed method?"

"My guess would be habit," Annan replied. "People in my father's time aren't that different from those now, once they have a method for doing something they change it only if if a new method can be shown to have some advantage over the old one. Anyway, regardless of how good or bad the method is, we must embrace it in order to use the archways."

"Is there an easy way to remember how many days each part of the year has?"

"The archway will not allow you to make an error, in that case. If you go beyond the maximum number of days in that part of the year, the counter will automatically switch to the next part and begin again from day one. However, most of this is immaterial. All you need to do return to the same place in time is memorise the numbers up here and re-enter them using the dials below once you have finished."

"And these lights select which of the portals we're in, right?" she asked, remembering what Medb had told her about the other portals and pointing at the controls marked 'Zones 1-5'.

"That's right. They represent the location of each of the other archways, allowing you to instantly travel to one of the different locations in whatever time you're in. Do you notice how the light with the symbol for five glows a little brighter than the rest? That's how you know which of the different archway locations you are currently at. If I was to press one of the other buttons, we would be immediately transported there."

"Why are there only five?"

"I have no idea. Perhaps, there are other groups of archways that are also interlinked, but from here we can only visit these."

"Surely your father must know, I mean, his time built the archways, didn't they?"

Annan looked at her, slightly puzzled. "Why would you think that? They are beyond even that time's knowledge."

"Then who did?"

"I don't know," Annan replied, "and neither does he, but someone from a time even further into the future than his own must have built them and sent them back into the past. That's the only way they could exist."

Annan spun the large dial to the right and Aife watched as they went forward in time at an alarming rate, with first hundreds, then thousands of years clicking past in front of her eyes. Eventually, Annan let go of the dial and the numbers stopped.

"Here we are," he said.

"Your father lives in the same place as your settlement?" Aife asked, surprised.

"Yes, though you might not recognise it..."

They stepped out of the archway into a dimly lit room, which reminded Aife a little of the portal itself. There were columns of black boxes with flickering lights, that covered most of the left hand wall and on the right large rectangular panels that also glowed faintly.

"What happened to the sky?" she asked Annan.

"We're underneath the ground" he replied, taking her hand. "Come with me." Annan led the way across the room and Aife dutifully followed. They were almost at the door when Aife saw something out of the corner of her eye, shrieked and drew her sword. There, in the far corner of the room stood two of the black shapes. They didn't move, but the line that bisected what would have been their faces glowed faintly. "It's ok," Annan reassured her, "They can't hurt you. You see how they're attached to the wall behind them? That's how they draw their power...they're charging."

"Charging?" Aife asked not comprehending what Annan was trying to tell her.

"Yes. It's like they are asleep."

"But what if they wake up?"

"They won't. They can't - not unless someone tells them to. Please, Aife, it's ok, they can't hurt you, I promise..." he took her hand once more and despite feeling uncertain, she followed him out of the room.

They found themselves in a small hallway in front of two closed metal doors. Annan pressed a small button next to the doors and it illuminated in much the same way as the panel in the archway portal. Aife heard a faint humming sound and then a muffled thump before the two metal doors slid open, revealing another, much smaller room beyond. Annan led Aife into the smaller room.

"But there's nothing here," she protested.

"Just wait a moment, you'll see," and he pressing one of another set of buttons on the inside of the small room.

The two metal doors closed again. Aife felt uneasy at being inside such a small space. Then she felt a slight jolt under her feet and the humming sound she had heard before began again, much louder this time and she felt a vague sensation of being pushed upwards.

"Look!" Annan made Aife turn away from the two metal doors towards the back wall of the small room. When they had entered, the back wall had been made of the same greyish stone like material as the rest of the walls in the hallway, but now Aife saw that it appeared to be moving past them quickly. In an instant the walls were gone and she found herself looking at huge towers that sprouted like mountains up into the sky. They were filled with lighted squares and in some of the nearer ones Aife could see the figures of people moving around inside. Up and up they climbed in the small metal room and Aife felt sure that eventually they would reach the very clouds themselves. They passed the tops of some of the towers and Aife could see an almost never-ending sprawl of further towers, also filled with lights and people. She could discern almost no trees or green whatsoever in this landscape and there was no sign of the river. However, the layout of the landscape told her that she was looking at what once had been the high tree lined valley that the river had cut through. She felt another slight jolt as their small room came to a stop and heard the double doors slide open behind her. A soft voice said something in a language she didn't understand. She turned and there was Morfran standing by the entrance to the little room. He was wearing loose fitting clothing and without the mask his face looker much kinder. His fair hair was tied back in a loose bun and whilst his scar still unnerved her, her overwhelming feeling when she looked at him now was one of pity, rather than fear.

"Aife can't understand you without the mask on, father," Annan said. "I know you find it hard to speak her language but please try."

Morfan's soft voice spoke once more. This time, although he spoke falteringly, Aife understood what he said:

"Can you still recognise it?" He asked, pointing at the view behind Aife.

"Aye," she replied,"it's so different though, but amazing...such structures...so many people. It scares me, yet it's also beautiful in its own way." Aife could see from his face that Morfran was having difficulty understanding what she had just said. Annan said something in the language she didn't understand. She guessed he was translating for her. Morfran nodded.

"Beautiful...but dying," he replied.

He pressed the buttons inside the small room, just as Annan had done. Then double doors slid shut once more and they descended back down to the hallway and room with the archway. He pressed a button on the wall and the dimly-lit room flooded with light. Aife saw the black shapes on the wall once more and recoiled.

"They cannot hurt you," a metallic voice said from behind her. She whirled around to see that Morfran once more had on the mask that covered the bottom half of his face. "Please, don't be alarmed. The mask turns the patterns of my speech into those of your language. The way we speak has altered a great deal since your time and much of the knowledge of how people spoke then has been lost. Annan has been teaching me as best he can, but as you heard, I'm not a very good student." Aife could see him smile a little under the mask, then he stepped in front of her and stood next to one of the black shapes. He reached up and tapped it sharply on its head. The shape did not react. "You see? Nothing. They are not real, not alive - at least as you understand it. They are machines, like a mill or a furnace. Does that make sense?"

Aife shook her head.

"But they look like people..." she said. She reached out and touched the shape. It felt cold and metallic. The shape did not stir. She slapped it with the palm of her hand, hard enough to make her skin sing. Nothing. Satisfied, she relaxed a little.

Morfran held out two masks, one for Aife and another for Annan. They were bigger versions of the one he wore, that covered the entire face.

"Please, put these on," he said. "You'll both need them where we're going."

Reluctantly, Aife put the mask on. She felt stifled by it. The sound of her breath in her ears almost deafened her.

"I don't like this," she said.

"It's ok, Aife," Annan said, looking at her and checking that the mask was on properly. "Just try to breathe normally. Can you hear me ok?"

Aife nodded. His voice sounded unnaturally loud inside the mask, as if he was shouting next to her ear.

Morfran took a pendant with the archways emblem from a shelf next them and they moved into the portal. Morfran twisted the large dial to the right for a few moments and then stopped. They emerged once more and this time Aife realised she was standing in water. They were still in the basement and Morfran lead them up some steps and out of the ruined apartment block.

"The air isn't as clean in this time," Morfran said as they looked out over the ruined landscape. "That's why we need the masks."

Many of the towers that Aife had seen before now lay in ruins. Everywhere she looked, the buildings seemed to be falling apart. Aife thought she could spot what looked like the skeletal remains of either humans or animals in places as well.

Everything was grey.

Everything was dead.

"This is 30 years forward from my time." Morfran said. Even through the mask, Aife could hear the sadness in his voice.

"What happened?"

"People and their selfishness happened. They went on taking and taking until eventually there was nothing left." From some of the derelict buildings, Aife could see ragged people start to emerge. "We need to leave," Morfran said, "it's not safe here..."

[2]

"So the world is dying?" Aife asked, once they were back in Morfran's time.

"That's right," Morfran replied, "my time still hopes they can save it. They don't realise that they're already too late."

"How did this happen?"

Morfan crossed to a control panel and pressed a few buttons. A light flickered behind him and front of Aife a small fire appeared, much like those she had made every night on her way downriver, except this seemed to float in mid-air. Instinctively, she put her hand to feel its warmth, but there was none. She moved her hand closer and closer until it disappeared through the flames. She yanked her hand back quickly, despite knowing that it had not been burnt as she had felt no heat whatsoever.

"It's not real," she said, putting her hands back into the flames once more, fascinated as they dancing around her fingers.

"It's like a painting," Morfran replied, "a painting that moves."

"Amazing..."

"This was the main way to get heat and energy in your time," Morfran continued. "You burnt wood to keep warm or to heat things for cooking or making stuff. When you burn something it converts the air around it into something else, that's what the smoke is. If you breathe it, you cough, because it's poisonous to us. After many hundreds of years of cutting down whole forests, we found even more poisonous things to draw heat and energy from." The image in front of Aife suddenly changed and she watched men with blackened faces and little lights on their hats working in a mine much like that in her settlement, except what they collected was a dull black stone. She saw this same stone pass along in hundreds of carts and saw it burnt it huge fires inside metal containers. She saw thick black smoke pour from thin towers and a landscape where the black smoke hung over it like a cloud. "Eventually, we found ways of making the light and heat work in every home, whenever you wished, all you had to do was press on a little button, like this..." Aife looked across at Morfran as he pressed something on the panel again and the image in front of her changed, once more. Now she saw rooms lit by small globes that hung from the ceiling and those same globes, only bigger, lighting rows of tall dwellings. The angle of the image changed and Aife saw that the row was only one in hundred other rows and those rows were only a small group in clusters of thousands of rows. She gasped at the scale of it all. "The quicker and easier the energy became, the more freely we used it. Not thinking that what powered it still had to come from somewhere." The image changed again and saw open green plains broken up with tall thin metal towers connected by wires; bigger towers, ones so huge she could barely believe that someone could build them, bellowing out white smoke this time, that was so huge it looked like they were making the clouds in the sky. She saw huge grey strips filled with metal objects, like covered carts, that people sat inside and moved by themselves and other groups of people climbing into a huge metal bird that took off into the sky. "We developed ways to move more quickly from place to place, all of which used energy. We used energy to leave the ground..." Now the image showed a huge white tower, taller even than those she had seen before which lifted itself off the ground in huge ball of flame. "...as well as to destroy it." The was a flash of light so bright, Aife closed her eyes to the image momentarily. When she opened them she saw the light had caused a cloud of smoke to rise up into the sky like a huge, evil-looking, black mushroom. She saw dwellings blown away like a piece of straw in the wind. "All of this poisoned the sky so much, that eventually, the world began to break down." She saw walls of water crash into dwellings, the ground shake and collapse under people's feet, huge forests of trees burning as far as the eye could see.

"Enough!" she said, at last. "I understand. We poisoned the world... how do we make it better?"

"There are lots possibilities that will work, the method is not the problem, the energy required to create it is." Morfran replied.

"I don't understand."

"All of the solutions need a form of power that can work again and again without needing more material. In order to do that we use the light of the Sun, but we still need a way of storing the energy that it creates. That's where you and your settlement come in." He led Aife over to a small display case, inside of which was a familiar looking, rose coloured crystal.

"Do you recognise this?" Aife nodded.

"It's the crystal we mine."

"We call this crystal, *Lepidolite*. Aside from its beauty it also has another purpose, a metal can be extracted from it. We call this metal: *Lithium*, until this crystal was discovered, no one believed that there were any places where it could be mined around here. Your father was wearing a pendant made of it when I met him, that's when I knew that he must come from or know where they were mining it." Morfran held up a small black brick. "Though it might not look like one, this is a power source." He pointed to the black shapes. "They are powered by one of these. Lots of things are. With enough of it you could use it to power something much bigger. It's a much better source of energy than burning wood or anything else, because it stores the energy from other sources like the sun and then keeps it locked away until you need it and when the energy inside is used up, you can use it again to store some more. There's just one problem: the crystal is fairly rare. To power the solutions needed to save our world we would need a lot of it. Most of it is owned by people who keep it for their own ends and who aren't interested in using it to help anyone else. Nobody from my time knows that there is this large natural deposit of it around here. That knowledge has been lost over time."

"So that's why you needed to find him again and my settlement? For the crystal that we mine there?"

"Yes. I only need to record the position of the mine so I can find it in my time, so it can be mined again. What I didn't count out on was having to spend many years trying to find him and your settlement again. That's why I was so desperate when I found you."

"What really happened between you two?"

"It's easier if I just show you. Come, it's time that you both saw this for yourselves..." He led Aife and Annan back to the portal.

(3)

This time he turned the large dial to the left and Aife watched as the numbers on the read out went backwards rapidly, past those from which she and Annan had come, before stopping some time earlier. Morfran pressed the button for Zone 1 and the three of them stepped out of the archway into a wood that, Aife guessed, must be somewhere in the hills above her settlement. As they moved nearer to where the edge of the wood opened out into a glade, Aife could see several figures staring out from the shadows towards the sunlit meadow beyond. As they got closer, she saw to her surprise that the figures all looked like Morfran.

"I've visited this same moment many times, wondering if I could have somehow changed what happened, but I soon realised that would be much too risky," he said in answer to Aife's surprised look. "The symbol on the keys is accurate. Time is not a straight line, it's a spiral that keeps looping back on itself. Once you've travelled back to this moment, a version of you will always be here, until you change that moment. These are the versions of me from those other visits. If you watch for long enough you'll see them each return to the archway and vanish. Keep to the shadows though, we don't want to be seen by anyone else."

They had reached the edge of the wood now and were looking out on the glade beyond. It was early evening. Aife could see a makeshift camp and a young man, about the same age as herself, whom she quickly recognised as her father, slowly building a fire. She heard a noise behind them and turned to see what must be a younger Morfran emerging from the archway. His clothes looked a little odd and he bore a strong resemblance to Annan. He stood by the archway for a few moments and studied it before heading towards the edge of the wood. He didn't see them hidden in the shadows as he walked past. Almost as soon as he stepped out from the trees he was spotted by Aife's father, who drew his bow immediately and aimed it at the young Morfran.

"Stop!" he shouted at the surprised Morfran, "Don't move!"

The young Morfran did as he was told and raised both his hands above his head.

"Who are you? What do you want here?" Aife's father shouted at him. The young Morfran didn't answer, he just stood there with his hands in the air. "What do you want here?" Aife's father repeated more forcefully this time.

"Why don't you answer him?" whispered Aife to the old Morfran, who stood beside her.

"I didn't know how to..." Old Morfran replied.

"But why didn't you have your mask with you?"

"Because I hadn't invented it yet."

The sudden swish of an arrow made Aife turn back towards the scene unfolding in front of her eyes. Her young father's arrow struck the tree directly beside young Morfran, who turned and fled back into the wood. Aife watched her father chase after him, already loading another arrow into his bow. The young Morfran's foot caught on an exposed root as he ran back towards the archway and he stumbled, his head striking a rock as he fell, creating the gash that scarred his face.

"It was an accident!" Aife cried, turning once more to old Morfran, who nodded. He put his finger to his lips and motioned to Aife to keep watching. She saw her father approach the wood with his bow raised. Once he saw young Morfran lying on the ground, not moving however, he lowered the bow slightly and approached slowly and cautiously. He nudged the prostrate young man slightly with his foot, but got no response.

"Hey, are you alright?," Aife's father asked, leaning down to shake the young Morfran's body this time. Aife thought she noticed a note of concern in his voice now. She saw the pendant that Morfran had mentioned, it was one she remembered from her childhood.

"How did you see the pendant if you were so badly hurt?" Aife whispered to Morfran.

"I only saw it when I came back to this moment afterwards, keep watching...." Aife turned back to see her father begin to look through young Morfran's pack. He held up various strange objects which Aife guessed must be from Morfran's time. Her father seemed equally puzzled by them and cautiously returned them to the pack. Then he found the sword, which he examined carefully. Finally, he removed the piece of lepidolite from the bag. Aife's father's expression changed from one of curiosity to fear.

Just then a sound came from the direction of the archway and Aife saw Medb appear, as if out of thin air. Her sudden appearance startled Aife's father and he dropped the piece of lepidolite and picked up Morfran's sword.

"There's no need to be afraid, I mean you no harm...what has happened here?"

"He ran... he must have fallen...I didn't mean to hurt him," Aife's father stammered, lowering the sword slightly.

"I understand," Medb replied, "but you must let me help him...he could be badly hurt."

"Stay back!" Aife's father shouted as Medb attempted to move towards him. He raised the sword again. "Where did you come from? One moment there was no-one there, now you're here...where did you come from?"

"I happened to be nearby, that's all..."

"That's not true! I've been travelling all through these parts, there are no settlements in that direction, so where did you come from? What about him?" Aife's father said, pointing towards the young Morfran. "Look at him! He doesn't look like he comes from nearby, look at his clothes and the things in his pack..."

Sensing the rising panic in the young man's voice, Medb stood still and spoke in even calmer tones than before. "It's alright, everything is going to be alright. Please, just let me help him." She moved towards him, slightly.

"No, stay back, I said." He backed away, almost stumbling over the same root that had caught young Morfran's foot. He regained his balance quickly though and then turned and ran. Aife watched her young father, Morfran's sword in his hand, running for his life. He crossed the glade without looking back and disappeared into the forest on the other side.

"I'm so sorry for what my father did. Here," she said handing the sword to Morfran, "this belongs to you."

"You keep it, Aife," he replied. "and there's nothing to forgive as far as your father is concerned; it was an accident and his reaction was understandable, given the circumstances."

Aife nodded and turned her attention back to the scene in the wood. Medb was tending to the injured young Morfran. She carefully repacked his things into the pack and dragged him back towards the archway. Once she got there, she removed another talisman from underneath her clothes and placed it around Morfran's neck. Then the two of them disappeared from view as they entered the portal.

Several of the other Morfrans then moved out from their hiding places and moved slowly back towards the archway. Some of them nodded to one another. Morfran waited until the last of them had gone through the archway before stepping out from behind the trees.

"You were very lucky Medb came along when she did." Aife said, now that the three of them were alone.

"I'm not sure luck had much to do with it." Morfran replied with a smile.

chapter nine:
future knowledge

O nce they returned to Morfran's time, he asked them both if they were hungry. Neither Aife nor Annan had had anything since that morning and happily agreed to the idea of something to eat. He led them both into the moving room once more and took them up to the top of the building, where his living quarters were. Just as before, Aife marvelled at the view from the windows as they travelled up to the penthouse, though that was to pale in comparison to her reaction to the inside of the penthouse itself, which offered an almost 360 degree view of the surrounding landscape with its floor to ceiling glass windows.

She spent at least ten minutes wandering from one window to the next, trying to take in every detail of what she saw. A passing drone startled her and she screamed thinking it was some form of giant bird or insect about to attack her, but Annan calmed her down and explained that it was simply a machine, like the black shapes.

"In the pictures you showed me, I saw that it was possible for people to fly like birds in this time, inside big metal tubes with wings...how wonderful that must be..." Aife said.

"I think most people take it for granted, these days," Morfran replied, "which is a shame, because it truly is wonderful."

Aife's attention turned to the middle of the room, where many, multicoloured square objects, of various sizes and thickness stood, stacked together in horizontal rows.

"What are these?," she asked.

"Books," Morfran replied and then, in response to Aife's puzzled expression, he added. "Collections of stories or histories, written down on paper." He walked over to where she stood, pulled a book from the shelf in front of her and opened it. "This one is about our bodies, it has pictures as well as writing." Aife's eyes widened at the illustrations that showed various details of human anatomy, the musculature, the skeleton.

"What's this, next to the pictures?" she asked, pointing to the text.

"That's writing," Morfran explained. "It's a little bit like the number system in the archways, only in this case the symbols make up words. In your time, language, that is words, were only spoken, changing slightly from one place to another but, eventually, people figured out how to write words down - so that their stories and histories might be passed on to other people, even those they didn't actually know or who lived long after they did."

"Do you have books with the stories and histories of my time?"

"Sort of..." Morfran led her to another section of the bookshelf. "These books here are about your time but they don't really tell your stories and histories, because what we have left are the remains of your buildings, weapons, pottery and so on. So much has been lost..."

"Lost how?"

"In just under a thousand years from your time, soldiers from another land will come to where you live. They will already have many things: weapons, tools, even a written language, that make them feel superior to your people. Little by little they will take over. Some of your people will fight them, some will try and live in peace with them, but because the soldiers language - their words - will be written down, much of the history of your people, which they do not consider important, will be forgotten. This will make it difficult for anyone later, say in my time, to really know what happened in yours."

"But why don't they use the portals? Then they could find out how things really were..."

"Most don't know about them, which is a good thing. By now, you must realise just how dangerous it would be if everyone knew about the archways. In my time, the actual archways have gone, leaving nothing to mark where the portals might be. Without that knowledge and more importantly, without a key, no-one would find them. My theory is that when the invaders from other lands destroyed much of the history and culture of your people they also, inadvertently, destroyed the knowledge of the portals as well."

"But you found them..."

"Yes, that's quite a long story, though...perhaps it can wait until we've finished eating."

With that he went back to preparing their food and Aife now became fascinated by the tools and devices used to prepare food in Morfran's time. No more open fires and dwellings filled with smoke, here everything seemed to be heated by little circles that glowed red. Aife was particularly taken with the shiny metal spout, from which water could be obtained with just a twist and even more so when Morfran showed her that the water that came out could be either hot or cold depending on which way the top was twisted.

Whilst Morfran was explaining this to her, he also asked her lots of questions about life in her settlement, seeming genuinely interested in her talk about the role of the council and slightly amused when she told him about Malvyn and Bricriu's duplicity and how they had manoeuvred her cousin Cahal out of the council and eventually convinced him to leave the settlement.

"I'm sorry," he said, seeing her frown, "it's simply that this Malvyn reminds me a great deal of many of the leaders in my time - they can't be trusted either."

"Are they ever punished for deceiving people in your time?"

"Sometimes, if there's enough people making enough noise about what they've done...but mostly it just gets quietly forgotten about. There's always people ready to believe the lies. In a way, it's almost comforting," he added with a wry grin, "no matter how much the language we speak or the tools that we use change, people are still the same."

"I don't see how that's a comfort."

"Because they're predictable and there is comfort in knowing that someone will always stand in your way, so get used to it and find ways to deal with it."

Aife realised that she needed to pee. She tried to ask Morfran how she could go outside in order to find a suitably quiet spot where she could do this, but he didn't really understand what she was asking him. Fortunately, Annan overheard the conversation, came to her rescue and explained that she didn't need to go outside and instead showed her to a small windowless room near the entrance.

"We do those things in here," he said, showing Aife the small, white room. He led her to the far end of the room and and a large, almost circular bowl, about knee height, with water at the bottom. "You sit on this and when you've finished doing whatever you need to do, you stand up and press this," he indicated a metal, circular section on the wall, behind the bowl, "and then the water takes everything away, like this..." He pressed

175

the metal circle and Aife jumped as more water flowed in from the sides of the bowl into the middle.

"Like a small waterfall," Aife said, astonished.

"And if you need to clean yourself, when you're finished, you can use this paper, here:" Annan showed her a circular roll of what looked like white cloth attached to the wall, next to the bowl. "You can put any paper that you use into the bowl and the water will take that away too."

"That definitely seems nicer than having to use leaves."

Annan laughed. "It is! In fact, you might find yourself wishing you never have to go back to using leaves again!" He then quickly showed her another smaller bowl, about waist height, which also had a metal spout with water, just like the one in the cooking area, where she could wash her hands afterwards.

Annan gave her some privacy and she lifted her tunic and sat down on the plastic seat of the toilet, which felt very strange underneath her. She particularly didn't like the way it shifted under her weight slightly from side to side. She finished as quickly as she could and then used a little of the white roll of paper and stood well back when the water flushed everything away, a little worried that, if she were too close, the water might try and take her with it.

Morfran and Annan were putting the food on the table when Aife came out of the bathroom and she happily sat down next to Annan as Morfran dished the food onto the plate in front of her. She was a little bemused by the fact that Morfran used metal utensils to eat his food with, but Annan told her not worry about it and just eat with her fingers as he did. She enjoyed the food Morfran had prepared: It was mostly vegetables (he explained that he didn't eat meat), some of which she recognised and others that she did not. She particularly enjoyed the large, white round ones, which Morfran told her were called "potatoes" and which, he informed her, wouldn't be introduced to the menu where she lived for over a thousand years after her time, when a famous explorer brought them back from another land separated from this one by a huge expanse of water, much larger than any river.

All this talk of distant times and other lands eventually prompted Morfran to tell Aife a little bit about his life and how he discovered the archways.

Firstly, just as Medb had told her, his name wasn't "Morfran" at all, but Matthew Francis (and Annan's wasn't really "Annan" but "Adam" - but had got so used to his new name, that his father now called him by it too). Aife, whose entire settlement only had one name each, wasn't sure why he needed two names and decided not to ask, as she was more interested in hearing about how he had discovered the portals.

He told her how his father had been someone who studied the things left behind by people from the past and how he'd discovered both the sword that Aife now had and the crystal he had shown her earlier amongst other objects in a burial place. He told her how the discovery of the sword had fascinated his father, how he'd known it was special and that the metal it was made of was unlike anything else normally found. He also told her about the dream he'd had of the man with the scarred face, who he later realised was an older version of himself, who gave him something called "co-ordinates"- special numbers that related to an exact location. He told her how he'd travelled to the same moment in the future where they had been and discovered what would happen if humans didn't stop poisoning the planet and how the older him had explained that finding the mine at Aife's settlement and recording its co-ordinates, so it could be found in his time could help change that.

"But earlier you said it was already too late to stop what was happening..."

"It is. The change would have to start from when I first discovered the portals, when I was your age. I would need to go back to that time and give them to my younger self, for there to be any hope of changing what happens."

"But wouldn't that mean changing everything? I mean, if you had already found the mine when you were younger, we wouldn't be sitting here now, would we?"

"Exactly. If my younger self has the co-ordinates to the mine then there would be no need for me to spend years searching for it in your time. I would never have needed to bring Annan there, perhaps I would have never even have met your father. Were that the case, perhaps many things in your life would have been different too. Your cousin might still be alive..."

"And what would happen to the version of us that exists now?"

"In all probability we will simply be gone. As if we never existed."

"But what about all the things that have happened, to you, me, Annan, Medb even...that would all be gone?"

"Yes, but you wouldn't know anything about it."

"You don't know that!"

"Well, I do...sort of. You see, that version of myself I met when I went into the future, that wasn't me, or at least the me that exists now, because in telling my younger self about the portals I changed the past. When I met your father, that too changed the past - for both you and me. You also changed your future when you stepped into the portal and went forward a year - who knows how different your life would have been otherwise... I realise that this is small comfort to this version of you who hasn't known anything other than this version of events, but it is important to know that this has already happened to you at least once and you knew nothing about it."

Aife got up from the table, shaking her head. "No, I'm sorry, I won't do it."

Annan was about to stand up and go over to her, but Morfran stopped him. He walked over to balcony doors and opened them.

"Come and look at this, Aife." he said to her.

Aife walked over to the edge of the balcony. The sun had set behind the hills, but there was still a little light in the sky. Stepping outside into the cool night air, Aife found herself dazzled once more by the beauty of the thousands of buildings and lights that lay stretched out in front of her, despite feeling uncomfortable about being up so high.

"Aside from being higher up, this the same view that you see from outside Medb's hut," Morfran said. "That hill, there, marks where the edge of the rock which surrounds her settlement used to be. Many years ago, I looked at that same view and had to make a choice: Spend my life with a woman I was in love with, wondering what might have been, or risking everything to make sure that all the people living there and all over the world had a chance of survival."

"Maybe it's not meant to survive - after all, if your time didn't build the portals, then something must have survived in order to do that. Why didn't they come back and change the past?"

Morfran sighed. "Perhaps they thought the same way as you - worried that if they changed the past then they wouldn't be here. You're absolutely right, of course. The world will survive, even though we and most of the animal life won't. Eventually, life will start again. It will be different than it is now and it might take thousands and thousands of years, maybe even longer than that, but it will do so - whatever future race of beings created the portals is proof of that. Though that won't help the billions who will lose their lives. When I was little, there was a slogan used by those who were worried about the world dying: There is no planet B. It was about the idea that humans couldn't just leave their problems behind and go and find another world and start again. Sadly, that's exactly what will happen. Those with wealth and power will escape into the sky in huge ships, as big as this building we're standing in now, whilst the poor will be left to fend for themselves in a dying world, where there's no food because most of the animal and plant life will have already died out. I know I'm asking you to care about something that doesn't directly effect you and that if we succeed, the world will be different for all of us, but it's not just our lives that are at stake here."

Aife looked across at him. She knew what he was saying was right, even though the thought of losing everything that was precious to her now: her time with Fionn, Medb and Annan - especially Annan - filled her with dread.

[3]

When Aife and Annan returned to their time, Medb and Fionn were exactly as they'd left them, as it was only mere moments beforehand that they'd said goodbye to them. Despite this, Fionn was clearly unhappy about Aife leaving her behind and gave a soft whine of greeting when she saw her friend approaching once more. Aife scratched the wolf behind her ears, which she knew she liked, and put her face close to the animal's.

"I'd like to be by myself for a little while," she said and then led Fionn through the wood to the small stream, where the two sat in silence, looking at the water. Lost in her own thoughts and busy fondling Fionn's soft fur, she was unaware of Medb until she was standing right beside her.

"He told you then?" Medb asked.

"I feel..." Aife struggled to find the right words to express her emotions, "as if I'm in the river, being pulled by a strong current towards a destination I'm not sure I want to visit."

Medb put her hand on Aife's shoulder. "I'm sorry for the burden that has been put on you, Aife. It's only natural that knowledge of the archways and of other times only enhances this feeling of no longer being in control of one's own life, but in a sense, everyone's future is decided for them: in the thousands of tiny decisions we each make, every day that we're alive, each day bringing us closer to our own inevitable demise. Morfran is trying to do what he believes is best, in order to save a lot of people. It's what has driven him for a great many years and naturally, he sees you as a means to making this happen."

"But will what Morfran intends to do actually make things better? Can you say for certain that it will?"

"No, but then we can say that about everything we try to do, can't we? What's important is that we try. There's never any guarantee that we will succeed, but if we don't try then we can only fail. Morfran's plan is risky and will have consequences that not even he can foresee, but that's less important than how many lives could be saved."

"Do you really believe that?"

"I'm staking my life on it," Medb replied and suddenly faded in and out of view in front of her. Aife jumped up as if stung, tripping over her own feet as she did so and landing back on the ground with a bump.

"W..w...what just happened?," she stammered, "how did you just disappear like that?"

"Calm down, Aife, I'm not going to hurt you. It's called temporal phasing, it's a little like what happens to you when you enter the archways."

Aife's eyes widened. "You're from the future! From the time that built the archways!"

Medb nodded. "Several thousand years after the last humans in this world have died, they return from out there... " she pointed upwards, "...living on other worlds. They are the descendants of those who lived here originally but launched themselves into the sky in search of new worlds to inhabit. Much of the knowledge about their old world has been lost and they are anxious to know more about their ancestors. Their machines have developed far beyond what was possible in Morfran's time. They developed "temporal phasing" as an easy way to move between different places and even different worlds and now they tried to adapt it to allow them to move through time to see and experience the history of their old world, but doing so was incredibly dangerous: Without enough knowledge of history to guide them there were many terrible accidents, with travellers ending up in the middle of battles and being killed on arrival. So, a new solution was found: temporal phasing was built into 5 devices, portals, spread over a relatively small area, especially chosen because nothing of great significance - no huge battles or events - ever happens there. It is literally, a "backwater" in terms of both time and place." Aife gasped and Medb smiled. "Yes, that is exactly how the name and the myth began for your settlement and many others around the river. This was the first settlement - all the others came from here. The portals were taken far into the past and left there. The travellers created the archways to mark them, so that they could find their way back and have special keys, some as pendants, some as other objects like swords, made so that only they could access the portals. There were only two important rules: Don't interfere with the events happening, and don't form close attachments or have children with those you meet in the past. Feeling safe that, in this way, they would neither alarm their distant relatives or risk altering important events, they were then free to explore the history of the world they had once come from, using knowledge gained from studying a small area over many thousands of years to understand how humankind developed. A little like studying a whole forest, by looking at one tree."

"But you altered events, didn't you?"

"Yes," Medb, sadly. "Even though, from a distance, a tree might look the same as many of the others, ultimately, it is unique and so are the people we meet in the past. Many of the travellers found that they could not remain objective about the fates of those they met and so started to change them. As a punishment, those travellers that do are forced to remain forever in the time they are studying, their keys taken away from them."

"But you still have yours..."

Medb shook her head. "Each traveller is given two keys. I gave one to Morfran in order for him to get home, the other was taken from me the day he left. When he brought me Annan to look after he gave me back the other key. By then, he'd managed to find another for himself. I don't regret it, I knew the risk I was taking. Once he told me what he was trying to do, I knew that I had to help him - no matter what the consequences. And there will be consequences, Aife - huge ones that not even Morfran has foreseen. If he stops humans from dying out, then there will be no need for them to return from other worlds and so the portals will never be built."

"But that means..."

"That the entire history of this area will change - there will be no myth of "backwater", because there will be nothing to start that myth..."

"Will you even exist if the world is saved?"

"I don't know."

"But then why let him go through with it, when you know it will change everything?"

"Because the fate all the people and animals who will die otherwise is still more important than my own."

"Does Morfran know that he might be sacrificing your life in order our to save the world?"

"No and neither does Annan and if you care for him as much as I think you do, then you'll keep it that way."

Aife found it hard to argue in the face of someone who was prepared to sacrifice so much in order to help people she would never meet.

chapter ten:
returning home

nnan and Morfran were waiting for them at the archway when they returned from the stream. Morfran was dressed in clothes from Aife's time so he would blend in a little better, and he'd covered his translator mask with a piece of cloth. Fionn was not yet convinced that Morfran could be trusted and growled softly about him being so near to her beloved friend, but Aife stroked her ears and told her it was alright. Morfran produced another pendant with a key and gave it to Aife hang it around the wolf's neck.

"I'm not sure it's a good idea to take Fionn with us - it will be harder for us to remain inconspicuous." Aife said.

"We have no idea what sort of welcome awaits us," Morfran replied. "I hope we can the record the position of the mine and then leave without being noticed, but from what you told me of the circumstances of you and your cousin's departure from your settlement, it may not be that simple. If it comes to a confrontation, we shall be glad to have Fionn by our side."

Fionn licked Aife's hand and looked up at her with a slight whine, as if to say: He's right, you know and even Aife eventually agreed it would be better to take her with them.

"Take care of yourself, my son," Medb said as she embraced Annan and then Aife. Then she turned to Morfran, who took his hands in hers. "Look after them, Matthew, don't risk too much."

"It feels as if I'm always saying goodbye to you," he said and hugged her tightly. Aife could see that there were tears in his eyes.

(2)

"You said Zone 1, where I met your father, was in the hills far above your settlement," said Morfran, "therefore the nearest archway to it must be either Zone 2 or 3."

"Have you been to both?" Aife asked him.

"Yes," he replied, "Zone 2 is near a small settlement, though it hardly seems big enough to be yours; whilst Zone 3 is in the forest high up above the river."

"The small settlement could belong to one of the outlier groups that we trade with. We should try that one first."

Morfran pressed the button for "Zone 2" on the portals control surface and then the four of them, with Aife keeping a tight hold of the fur at the back of Fionn's neck, ventured outside.

They found themselves in a small wood and once they got to the edge of it, Aife realised she had been correct and that they were close to one of the outlier settlements, not far from her own.

"My settlement is this way," she said, pointing more or less due east.

"We must go carefully," Morfran replied, "we don't want to attract any undue attention - after all, we don't know what sort of reaction your return will create."

"Well, we don't need to worry about that here," said Annan, "there doesn't seem to be anyone around."

"Aye, that's odd," said Aife, "the two of you wait here a moment..." She motioned for Fionn to stay with the others and then she went to the nearest of the outlier buildings. There was no sign of anyone. She went to another building and then another - still nothing. In the fourth, she found food left on the table, its rotten state told her that the occupants had been disturbed during their meal some time ago and had not returned since.

"Something strange has happened here," she said as she returned to the others. "The buildings have all been deserted and it looks like the people left in a hurry."

Morfran returned to the portal and a few moments later returned carrying two weapons as well as two black boxes, which he placed on the ground next to the archway. He gave one of the weapons to Annan, as well as a small handheld device.

"What's that?" Aife asked him.

"Just a precaution. Come on, let's get moving."

[3]

It took them some time before they reached the edge of Aife's settlement and mindful of what Morfran had said about being cautious, she deliberately led them a way that would keep them hidden for the most part, approaching it from the woods below the right hand side of the waterfall. Manoeuvring quietly through a small clump of trees, very near the spot where Aife had sat and watched the sunrise after her father's death, they were able to get a clear view of the entrance to the mine.

"The mine's over there, in a cave hidden under the waterfall." she told Morfran.

He produced something from his pocket that looked like two small black cylinders joined in the middle and put them to his eyes.

"Hmm...can't really see whether there's anyone by the entrance from here," he said, "as the waterfall obscures it too much...no, wait, I can see something moving. Here take a look.....they make things far away seem as if they're much nearer to you..."

Aife took the binoculars and put them to her eyes as he had done. "It's like we're right next to it!" she gasped, training them on the entrance to the mine. "Yes, there's someone bringing crystals from the mine now...that's strange..."

"What is?" Morfran asked.

"They seem to be loading them onto a series of small carts. I don't remember them doing that before..."

"May I see?"

Aife handed the black cylinders back to Morfran and he looked through them again. Now it was his turn to gasp.

"What is it?"

"We need to get a closer look at those carts."

There wasn't much in the way of trees to hide them as they approached the mine. As they hid behind the last sizeable clump of trees, nearest the mine entrance, Morfran reached for the black cylinders, once more. Aife could tell that something was troubling him. He handed the black cylinders to Annan and pointed towards the small carts.

"But that's impossible!" Annan said, after looking through them at what his father had indicated.

"Far from it, but it's disturbing."

"What's wrong?" Aife asked again.

"Those carts are something that shouldn't be here, in your time." Annan replied. "We should leave," he said to his father, "take your measurements and let's get out of here before someone sees us and ruins the whole plan."

"I need to get closer. Annan, stay here with Fionn." He handed him his weapon. "Aife and I will go up towards the mine entrance and get the measurements."

Annan nodded. Fionn whined slightly as she realised that Aife was leaving her behind once more, but seemed reassured by Annan stroking her and telling the wolf that Aife would soon return.

Keeping as low as they could, Morfran and Aife crept towards the mine entrance. Once there, they crouched down behind the small silver carts, which Aife now realised ran on small black lines all the way up the slope. Morfran took a small black box from his inside his clothes and held it up in front of him.

"I need a few seconds for it to make the calculations," he said. Aife watched as the black box whirred softly and images and numbers slowly appeared on its surface. "Good, we're done, let's go back to Annan."

They began to move away but suddenly Morfran stopped. He had spotted part of a motif stuck to the side of one of the small carts and ran his fingers over it. Almost as if in reaction to this gesture a shout rang out above them and Aife turned to see a group of men, armed with similar looking weapons to those of Morfran and the black shapes, moving down the slope towards them. She looked at Morfran to see whether they should try and make a run for it, but he put his hand up and signalled for her to stay calm. She saw him remove the small black box and place it underneath the carts and then look towards the place where Annan was hiding and nod. Then he stood up and raised his hands in a gesture of surrender. As the group of men drew nearer, Aife recognised both Anghus and Eghan.

"What are you doing here?" Eghan asked, once he drew level with Aife and Morfran.

"Eghan it's me, Aife."

"That's not what I asked - what are you doing here?"

"We've come to see the person in charge of this settlement," Morfran replied, "will you take us to them?"

"Not until you tell me what you were doing by the mine." Eghan said, raising his weapon.

"Take it easy, Eghan," said Anghus, stepping between him and Morfan and pushing Eghan's weapon down as he did so. "They're not attacking us. Let's search them for weapons and then take them to the broch, they can explain themselves there."

"I don't like it, they should tell us what they're doing here."

"Like it or not, I'm in charge here, not you. Check them for weapons and take them to the broch, is that clear?"

Eghan nodded, looking down at the ground. Aife was glad to see Anghus was still respected amongst the settlement. He searched Morfran and then turned to Aife.

"Is that really you, Aife?," he asked as he removed her sword.

"Aye, Anghus, it is."

"It's good to see you again, but you should not have come back here. The two of you had better come with me." With that, he led Aife and Morfran back up the slope towards the settlement. Eghan and the others followed behind.

As soon as he was sure they were well out of sight, Annan stole over to the carts and collected the little black box from where he is father had dropped it.

[4]

If Annan had stopped to look at the side of the cart as he collected the black box from underneath it, he too might have recognised the faded, but nonetheless distinctive, motif, still visible on the side: a letter "B", stretched out so that it resembled a stylised drawing of a bird's wings - the company logo of Benway Industries, a large, multi-national conglomerate owned by billionaire, George Benway, one of the ten richest people in the world.

Beginning in the field of computers, Benway had made had already become a millionaire aged just seventeen, when his first ever company was bought by Google. He then diversified into the energy and aeronautics industries, increasing his fortune still further. He became notable by providing sustainable solutions for clean water in drought stricken regions of Africa and his attempts to abolish child poverty. His many charitable foundations, supporting everything from free computers and tablets, full scholarships for disadvantaged children and grants to firms advancing green energy were well known, but controversy dogged him too. He'd been the subject of several breach of privacy lawsuits, because his software could potentially be used by governments to spy on ordinary citizens -

some said this was deliberate and that he had a great deal of influence not only within the government but the military, as well. It was certainly true that none of the lawsuits were ever successful. Charges were dropped, people recanted their testimonies, evidence and sometimes even witnesses went missing and Benway walked away unscathed.

Despite much publicised environmental activism, it was also strongly rumoured that he was secretly buying up land and resources throughout the globe, slowly building a monopoly of natural gas and water reservoirs.

More importantly, he also owned or had some stake in the majority of lepidolite being mined worldwide. Which is why Morfran immediately recognised the logo on the mining carts and why he showed little or no surprise when he and Aife were ushered into the central chamber of the council broch, to find George Benway sitting at the other end atop a large wooden throne, surrounded by a bunch of heavily armed men and Bricriu.

"Matthew? What on earth are you doing here?" Benway asked with a grin.

"I might ask you the same question, George," Morfran replied. "You don't look that surprised to see me."

"In truth, I'm not. In fact, I've been expecting you..." Benway replied, smiling. He got up from his throne and came forward to meet them with Bricriu and two of his guards.Aife noticed that he and his bodyguards had on translator masks just like Morfran. "Did you search them?" he asked Anghus.

"She had her sword, otherwise they were unarmed."

"Make sure they didn't bring any friends with them..." Benway replied and Anghus gestured to Eghan and the other guards that they should go and check.

"You know him?" Aife asked Morfran.

"Oh Matthew and I go back quite a few years..." Benway replied before Morfran could answer. "And who might you be?" he asked Aife. "It's ok, you can talk - there's no need to be afraid of me..."

"My name is Aife and I'm not afraid of you."

"Wow! She's got some spirit, clearly," he said, turning to Bricriu and his guard.

"She is from here, originally," Bricriu replied, "her father was one of the council until his death. She left the settlement under a cloud over a year ago and hasn't been seen since."

"Interesting..." Benway said, looking Aife up and down. "Why did you have to leave? Didn't everyone find you charming and cute?"

"I didn't have to leave, I chose to. Later on, Bricriu and Malvyn decided to tell lies about my cousin and myself to hide their own treachery."

Benway laughed. "It doesn't look like she's very fond of you, my friend," he said putting his arm around Bricriu's shoulders - a gesture that even Aife could see Bricriu found uncomfortable. "Well, you're certainly right about one thing, Aife, and that's that Bri here is a conniving son of a bitch, then again, if he wasn't I never would have found this place. I was lucky enough to cross paths with him whilst he was looking for settlements trade your lepidolite with. I persuaded him to bring me here to meet with their chief, a man called Malvyn, and the rest, as they say, is history."

"So your treachery has finally gained its reward, eh Bricriu?" Aife asked him. "And where's Malvyn? Why isn't he here to enjoy the fruits of your labours?"

Bricriu looked away. "Regrettably..." he began.

"He's dead," said Oriana in a loud voice, as she entered the chamber and strode over to where they all stood. "I'm in charge of this settlement now, along with George..."

"It seems like you've gotten everything you ever wanted." Aife replied."

"You shouldn't have come back. She was always jealous of me," she announced to the others, "that's why she left. She couldn't bear the fact that her cousin and I were in love and when she found out we were due to be married, she tried to poison him against me by making up lies about my father."

"That's not true! Malvyn and Bricriu were the ones who lied when they tried to deceive the council and when Cahal tried to expose them, they made up more lies about him and I so that he had to leave the council and this settlement. You never loved Cahal, you were simply using him to safeguard your standing in the settlement. As soon as he was no longer of any use to you, you dropped him like a stone!"

"Who told you that?" Oriana shouted.

"Cahal told me that himself, before he died."

Oriana slapped Aife across the face, "Hold your tongue or I'll have you killed this instant!"

"Wow!," said Benway, coming between the two women. "Clearly some history between these two! Maybe we should let them fight it out like gladiators and let everyone watch, huh?" He turned to Aife. "So why did you decide to come back, when you knew you wouldn't be welcome?"

"I came to help Morfran save this world."

Another roar of laughter from Benway, with Oriana joining in this time. "What do you care about what happens to a world when you and everyone you care about will be nothing but dust by that time?"

"The fate of the world is something we all need to care about. Didn't they teach you that where you come from?

Benway's smile faded once more. "I can see why you weren't very popular here."

"How did you even find the portals, George?" Morfran asked in an attempt to deflect attention away from Aife by changing the subject. "I only stumbled on them by accident."

"Well, that's the funny thing, you see, after you approached me about purchasing shares in my lithium mines, a man came to see me. He told me a very interesting story, about how your father discovered lepidolite at a bronze age dig and your own collection of memorabilia, including many pieces with this same symbol," he touched the pendant around Morfran's neck, "made of a very rare metal - one whose composition shouldn't exist, at least not on this planet. He told me all about your plan to uncover a lepidolite mine that had been forgotten about for thousands of years and then he gave me a pendant like yours and a set of G.P.S. co-ordinates. When I went to their location, guess what I found? A portal through time."

"And your first instinct on discovering this amazing thing was to use it to steal stuff from the past. How noble of you, George."

"I don't need any morality lessons from you, Matthew! I haven't seen you using the portals to help your fellow man throughout history. We're exactly the same you and I - the only difference is that while you were busy taking your time, I snuck in under your nose and starting doing the very thing you planned to do!"

"I wasn't planning to steal the lepidolite from them though, George. I just wanted its location to find it in our time. Did you even think about what sort of a cataclysmic change you've wrought on history by doing this?"

"In less than a thousand years the Romans will wipe this place clean, you know that as well as I do. There will barely be a trace of this civilisation left behind afterwards"

"Things might be a little different now you've armed them with the latest weaponry. The Romans won't stand much of a chance against them, will they?"

"Ha! Yeah, part of me would really like to see that happen, you know..." He leaned in close so only Morfran and Aife could hear what he was saying. "Just between us, I'll be making sure that there's no one left to tell any tales on me by the time I leave, just to be on the safe side."

"Even by your standards, that's pretty insane, George. Think how many people throughout history will never exist if you do that."

"What do I care? I'm not from around here."

"What about your grandparents or their grandparents, George? How far back did you check?"

Benway just laughed. "This whole planet is dying, uninhabitable to humans and most wildlife species in 30 years from our time and that's what you're worried about? Whether a few people are not going to exist?"

"You own more lithium than anyone else, George. Why not use it to change the fate of this world, just as I'm trying to?"

"Who do you think is actually going to save a large chunk of humanity, Matthew? You? With some green energy solution or some hypothetical scheme to re-ionize the oceans or recycle CO2? No, it'll be me, taking as many as I can on rockets so that humankind doesn't die out along with this planet, so that eventually we can come back and build the portals that end up bringing us back here to the past!"

"And who decides which specimens of humanity get to leave? Will you be playing 'Noah', selecting the animals two-by-two? Or will the criteria be something much simpler, like who can afford to pay for the privilege of survival?"

"Scoff all you like, Matthew, this isn't a "what if" any more, this has already happened - the portals prove that. I just need to make sure it all goes to plan. Sadly, it's a plan that doesn't include you or your young friend here, but then you should know by now what happens to those who try and get in my way..." He turned to Anghus. "Keep them locked up until dark, then take them both down to the river and get rid of them. Make sure their bodies are washed far downstream, I don't want anybody asking questions about them."

Aife could see Oriana grinning to herself as Anghus and the other guards took her and Morfran to the place where prisoners were kept - a small dark cell, near the entrance to the broch - and pushed them inside.

The cell had single narrow slit in the door, which provided what little illumination that there was inside. It took Aife's a few minutes to adjust to the near darkness before she realised that she and Morfran were not the only captives being held there.

"Aife? Is that really you?" called a voice from out of a dark corner.

"Aye," Aife replied. "Who is it? Come a little closer so that I can see you..."

A figure stumbled towards them out of the darkness.

"Ethne?" she asked, shocked by the appearance of her friend.

Dirty and dishevelled, her face showing obvious signs of having been badly beaten, Ethne seemed a frail ghost of her former self. She recoiled in fright when she saw Morfran, standing next to Aife.

"It's ok," Aife told her, "he's a friend."

Ethne limped over to where they stood and almost collapsed into Aife's arms.

"Ethne, what happened? who did this to you?"

Ethne just smiled deliriously at her, revealing several broken teeth.

"The guards actually did it but you can guess who ordered it...she even stood there and watched - told me she was teaching me a lesson and making me prettier at the same time."

"But what had you done?"

"Oh, you know, the usual. I told that vile bitch what I thought of her...my own fault really. Everyone knows she killed Malvyn, but no one dares to say it out loud."

"She killed her own father?"

"And Ferghus too when he stood in the way of her being with Benway."

"But why didn't Anghus or someone try and stop her?"

"Because he's scared. They're all scared. If anyone stands up to Benway, then their families are killed. That's what they've done to anyone who's tried to stand against them - killed their wives and children and made them watch. They did the same with the outliers when they brought them here to work in the mine... after a while, nobody dared fight them."

Angry, Aife turned on Morfran. "This is your doing," she said, "Benway wouldn't have even known about the mine if hadn't been for you!"

To her surprise he didn't even try to argue with her. "Yes, it's all my fault...what has happened to your settlement...what happened to Annan's mother - all of it."

"That's what Benway meant when he said that 'you should know what happens to people who get in his way' - he killed Annan's mother?"

"He killed them both. Some years ago, worried that I would never be able to discover the location of your settlement, I tried to buy shares in lithium mines in order to be able to slow down the world's destruction. Benway owns the majority of the mines, so it made sense to approach him. I even offered him the patent on the translator masks I'd invented. He refused, of course, and then stole the design anyway. Then he arranged an accident. It was meant for me, but instead Claire and Annan were killed."

"You went back and tried to save them..."

Morfran nodded, tears now rolling down his cheeks.

"You couldn't save them both?"

"No matter what I tried...eventually it became clear that I would have to let him believe they were both dead and the only way to do that was bring Annan here. I sacrificed being a parent, so that my son would have a chance to live." He broke down sobbing. "All this time, I'd assumed it was something I'd said that had put their lives in danger, but now I know I was betrayed."

"The man who gave Benway the pendant and co-ordinates - but who was that?"

"Isn't it obvious? Someone who doesn't want the world to be saved - because then they wouldn't exist."

"The people who built the portals."

"Exactly, which means we're in even more danger than we thought. I'll tell Annan that he needs to head back to the portal with the compass right now. He can wait for us there, but if we're not back and hour after sundown he should go without us."

"But how will you be able to tell him?"

"With this..." He pulled apart one of the bracelets he was wearing, revealing a small device with a screen that lit up as soon as he touched it. "You don't think I'd give up all my tricks, do you?"

chapter eleven:
fights in the dark

annan was still crouched in more or less the same place as the three of them had hidden earlier whilst observing the mine entrance. Fionn sat dutifully at his side. The two of them had needed to shift their position slightly, from time to time, to avoid being spotted by one of the many patrols that constantly swept through the settlement. After he'd collected the locator device his father had dropped, he'd returned here, knowing that he'd be expected to wait for a signal of some kind. It had taken a while and Annan had begun to worry. What if the guards had killed Aife and his father before they'd had a chance to get him a message? He had to keep telling himself that if the guards had simply wanted to kill them they would have done so immediately. The fact that they were taken prisoner meant that someone would want to question them, so there was still a chance that they were both ok.

From what he'd seen of the guard patrols it was clear that whoever had taken control of the settlement had brought a heavily armed contingent with them. Their plasma rifles were the same type that the black shapes were armed with. He and his father had brought smaller variants with them, but Morfran had left his with Annan, when he went over to the mine. He suspected he could take out one patrol, at least, with the two weapons and Fionn, but he wasn't sure how many more there were and anyway, a rescue attempt was useless when you didn't know exactly where the people you needed to rescue were. So, instead he was forced to keep Fionn and himself hidden and wait. He was just beginning to wonder whether or not he and Fionn should try and get a little closer to the mine when a message appeared on his wrist device.

Aife and I are safe for now. The settlement is being held by George Benway and a group of armed mercenaries. They plan to dispose of us down by the river once it gets dark. When they do, we will make our escape and meet you back at the portal. If we are not back at the portal three hours after sundown, take the compass and go back to the moment I met Aife's father and give the co-ordinates on it to my younger self - he must make a note of the co-ordinates himself, otherwise you and the compass will both disappear once you change the past. On no account attempt to rescue us - the most important thing is the information held in that device. It must be delivered safely to my younger self, otherwise all this has been for nothing.

Fionn gave a little whine next to him as if to say she was worried about Aife too.

"I know," he said stroking the wolf's soft white fur, "but don't worry - they're ok and we'll see them again soon, you'll see. Come on, we need to get moving."

[2]

After what seemed like an extremely long time, Aife noticed the light coming in through the slit of the cell door, fade and eventually be replaced by the orange glow of a burning torch outside. Soon afterwards she heard footsteps outside the door and signalled to Morfran to get ready.

The door opened and there stood Oriana with Anghus, Eghan and two other guards that Aife didn't recognise.

"Pull them out of there and let's get on with this," Oriana ordered.

The guards hustled Aife and Morfran out of the cell and were about to close the door again, when Oriana changed her mind and told them to bring Ethne along as well.

"Might as well get rid of all of the troublemakers at the same time," she said with a thin smile.

"And there I was thinking that you didn't love me anymore." Ethne's snide retort earned her a clout to the back of her head from Eghan's weapon.

"That's enough!" shouted Anghus when Eghan raised his weapon to hit Ethne a second time.

"Who are you to say what my brother should or should not do?" Oriana snapped back at him. "Hold your tongue or you and your family will suffer. Hit her again, Eghan!" and he did so with enough force that Ethne fell to her knees.

"I swear," she said to Oriana with look of fury in her eyes, "that will be the last time, you or anyone else is ever going to hit me."

"You're right," Oriana replied, "because soon you'll be dead. Get her on her feet and let's get moving."

Once outside the council broch, the three prisoners were led back down the slope and past the mine and through the trees to the river bank beyond.

"You seem to be well practiced at this, Oriana," Aife asked as they were led further into the trees that ran alongside the riverbank. "How many others have you quietly made to disappear like this?"

"Enough to know no one will miss you when you're gone."

"What about Malvyn? Didn't anyone miss him?"

Oriana didn't answer. She made sure they were well out of sight of the mine and then told them to stop a few feet from the water's edge.

"This will do," she said to Anghus and the others. "We can push them into the water once we're done and the current will take their bodies downriver."

The guards all took aim and just at that moment they heard the sound of someone moving through the trees behind them. Oriana and the guards all turned as

Idelisa, dressed in a long cloak, walked over to where they stood.

"What do you think you're doing here?" Oriana asked, irritably.

"I came to say goodbye to my friends, surely not even you can object to that?" Idelisa replied before going over to Ethne and embracing her. Then she turned to Aife and did the same. As she did so, Aife felt Idelisa thrust something into her hand from underneath her cloak.

It was the sword!

She looked up at Idelisa's face, dumbfounded, only to see her old friend wink back her. Aife quickly shifted the sword behind her back.

"Alright, that's enough!" Oriana shouted, coming between the two of them. "You've said your goodbyes now be on your way..."

"As you wish..."

Oriana turned away from Aife slightly, watching as Idelisa moved away. Aife saw her chance and took it. She pulled Oriana in front of her bringing her sword up to her throat as she did so.

"Put down your weapons!" Aife shouted at Eghan and the other guards, "or I'll cut her throat!"

"Don't listen to her, kill the other prisoners!" Oriana replied.

"I wouldn't do that if I were you." Anghus said. He had his knife at Eghan's throat, just as Aife had her sword to Oriana's. Idelisa took Eghan's weapon and pointed it at the other two guards.

"Put down your weapons!" she shouted at them. They wisely did as they were told. Morfran picked them both up and handed one to Ethne.

"So what now?" Oriana asked defiantly, "Are you going to kill us or take us back to the settlement and make Benway surrender?"

"There would be no point in that," Morfran replied, "he doesn't value your life more than anyone else's. He would have killed you himself when the time came."

"That's a lie!" Oriana shouted at him.

"It's not," Aife said. "Once he'd mined all the crystal he could he would have killed everyone in the settlement, including you. He admitted as much to Morfran and myself."

This seemed to cause a change in Oriana's attitude. Somehow, even she seemed to realise that this was the truth.

Ethne walked walked over to Oriana and punched her in the face. "Who's the pretty one now?" Ethne spat, as blood flowed readily from Oriana's nose. But the blow had loosened Aife's grip on her and that was the opportunity Oriana had been waiting for. She elbowed Aife in the ribs and kicked Ethne in the stomach. Breaking free, she drew the dagger she carried around her waist and lunged at Aife, but missed her. Morfran tried to seize Oriana but she slashed at his belly, cutting him deeply, and then dashed off into the trees.

All hell broke loose.

Aife ran after Oriana and Morfran followed as best he could. The two guards reached for their swords but were blasted into oblivion by Idelisa. Eghan tried to do the same thing as his sister but he had little chance against Anghus and he twisted in the big man's grasp, Anghus' knife came up and deftly sliced open his throat.

Morfran caught up with Aife by the river's edge. There was no sign of Oriana anywhere.

"Let her go, Aife," he said taking hold of her arm, "She has nowhere to go and we need to return to the portal..."

"What if she warns Benway?"

"We'll be ahead of him - that's why we need to go now, so we can make sure we fix all of this."

"You're hurt," she said, indicating the wound in his side.

"I'll manage...but we need go now, Aife, please..."

Reluctantly, Aife nodded and the two of them headed back to join the others.

"What happened to Oriana?" Anghus asked when they returned.

"She got away."

"Then we must move against Benway now, before she can raise the alarm. We must meet Henwas and the others at the mine and free the prisoners."

"It sounds as if you've been planning this for a long time." Aife replied.

"We have," said Idelisa. "We just needed an opportunity. When Anghus told me you'd returned, I knew it would be the best chance we'd have."

"You planned this?" Aife asked.

"Along with Ethne, my mother and most of the other women in the settlement. We were the only ones who could. The men were working as guards or in the mine. Benway and Oriana were watching them all closely, but they thought they didn't need to bother with us."

"Oriana should have known that the women here are more dangerous than the men," Ethne added, "but she was far too busy trying to secure power for herself."

"And there I was thinking that Aife here was exceptional, now I see where it comes from," said Morfran with a weak smile.

"But she was the first," Ethne replied, "she was the one who inspired us. We all knew that if she'd been here, she would have fought both Benway and Oriana."

"I'm so sorry I left you all," Aife said. "I shouldn't have gone. If I'd stayed, maybe none of this would have happened."

"It's not your fault," Idelisa said, putting her arm on Aife's shoulder. "You couldn't have known. Is it true what Anghus told me? Cahal is dead?"

Aife nodded. "He died saving my life."

"And mine," Morfran added. Aife looked up at him, surprised, and saw that he meant what he said. "He was a brave man. We must not let his sacrifice be in vain."

"We'll make sure of that," said Anghus. "but we must meet up with Henwas, before it's too late. Come on, let's go."

Aife and Morfran hung back as the others turned to go.

"We can't come with you," Aife said.

"But we need you," Anghus replied, "the whole settlement knows you've returned. They expect you to lead them against Benway."

"You don't need me to lead you. You already have a leader - more than one, in fact..." she said, indicating Idelisa and Ethne.

"Aife is right," Morfran said. "For us to really defeat Benway, we must divide ourselves into two forces. You and the settlement must stop him here. Aife and I need to make sure the damage he's already done is repaired."

"But how can you do that?" Idelisa asked.

"It's too difficult to explain," Aife replied, "but it's important for us to make sure neither he nor anyone else like him can come here and harm us. Our settlement is not the only thing at stake here."

Idelisa nodded. She took Aife in her arms and embraced her. "Do what you need to do," she told Aife, "we'll be waiting here for you when you return."

Ethne hugged Aife as well and Anghus took Morfran's hand in his.

"Thank you for bringing Aife back to us," he said, "may the spirit of the ancestors aid you in your endeavour."

"And you in yours," Morfran replied. "Rest assured, I will not rest until I have repaired the damage done by Benway and his men, you have my word on that."

Having said their farewells, the two groups moved off in their different directions, unaware that they were being watched. Once she was sure Ethne, Idelisa and Anghus were gone, Oriana stepped quietly out from where she'd been hiding and began to follow Aife and Morfran.

[3]

By the time Aife and the others were fighting with Oriana and the guards at the river's edge, Annan and Fionn had almost made it back to the portal. As they approached the entrance to the small wood, however, Fionn let out a low growl.

"Is someone there?" Annan shouted as he drew the weapon from underneath his cloak.

Then to his surprise, Medb came to the entrance of the wood. Annan lowered his weapon and was about to run forward to greet her when Fionn growled once more. Annan stopped in his tracks.

"What's wrong, Mother? What are you doing here?"

"Nothing's wrong," she replied stiffly. "Why should anything be wrong? Where are the others?"

Something in her tone of voice made Annan suspicious. He lifted the weapon slightly.

"They'll be here soon. They were waylaid slightly at Aife's settlement."

"Did they manage to record the position of her settlement on your father's device?"

"Yes."

"Who has the device?"

"Well, I do but..."

"Give it to me."

"What? Why?"

"Give it to me, Annan...it's important."

Annan stiffened at this. Fionn growled again.

"No," he replied.

"Please, Annan. You need to do as I tell you."

Annan pointed the weapon at her. "My real mother wouldn't ask for it, who are you?"

A figure in white stepped out from the shadows behind Medb. It was clear he was holding some sort of weapon to Medb's back. Two other armed figures dressed in white materialized out of thin air, on either side of Annan and Fionn. The wolf's growl became a snarl.

"Do as your mother asks, lad," Kynthelig said, "that way no one needs to get hurt."

"Why do you want it? What possible use is it to you?"

"I don't want to use it," Kynthelig replied, "I only want to make sure that your father doesn't."

"He's trying to save millions of people."

"But others, including myself and your mother, here, will never be born if he succeeds."

"Is this true?" Annan asked Medb, shocked.

She nodded. "It's sacrifice I'm willing to make," she replied.

"But I'm not." Kynthelig interrupted.

"So that's it?" Annan asked him. "You're putting your own life ahead of the millions of human beings and other living things that will die if we don't stop what's happening to the world?"

"I tried to stop your father with gentler means before, several times. It didn't work, so I was forced to resort to more drastic measures, like the accident that claimed your birth mother."

"You killed my mother?"

"Not personally, but I was responsible for suggesting that an accident befell your family. One that should have killed both you and your father as well. Unfortunately, things didn't go as planned, but for a while it seemed as if I had achieved my objective nonetheless - your father gave up his search for the location of the mine."

"Until Aife came along..."

"Exactly. The one variable I hadn't counted on: that someone who knew of the mine would find him."

"So if he does give the co-ordinates of the mine to his younger self, he will actually succeed in changing the future?"

"Yes, which is why I need you to give me the compass."

"And if I refuse?" Annan asked. He saw the two men on either side of him come a little bit nearer. Fionn had lowered her shoulders slightly, ready to pounce. She would happily fight alongside him if need be.

"Don't refuse," Kynthelig replied. "You're outnumbered. It would be...a mistake."

Annan removed a small box from beneath the folds of his cloak and held it out in front of him. Kynthelig released his grip on Medb and came towards Annan.

"You're the one who made the mistake," Annan said, as he approached him, "when you killed my mother."

He pressed a button on the box and Kynthelig stopped in his tracks. The man on Annan's left took aim with his weapon and fired, but the blast ricocheted off one of the two black shapes that unfurled themselves from the black boxes that Morfran had placed on the ground a few hours before. Annan's would-be-assailant looked in horror as the black shape turned its menacing, featureless face in his direction.

"Let's see who's outnumbered now?" Annan shouted angrily as he and the black shapes charged the group of men in white with Fionn leading the way with a snarl so ferocious that the trees of the wood shook from the sound.

George Benway lay on his straw bedding, in his chamber in the upper level of council broch, waiting for Oriana to return. She had been gone awhile. Since the council had been disbanded there were no other families living there, he resided almost alone, with her. Mostly, it was only Bricriu, who had no wife and children, and Benway's personal guard who were allowed in the building at night. Oriana had even sent her brother to live with some of their relatives after her father's death, something Benway was secretly glad about. He didn't like the possibility of Eghan deciding to attack him in his sleep, when he'd had a bit too much to drink and decided that Benway needed to answer for his father's death. Much better that he remain at arm's length, like the rest of the settlement.

Whilst Eghan might have felt justified in directing his wrath towards the modern interloper, it wasn't Benway who had been chiefly responsible for Malvyn's death. Ethne had been correct - it was Oriana who had done the deed. The two had planned it together, of course, the simplicity of it having appealed to George, especially in a time where there were no autopsies to complicate matters; but he wasn't one who enjoyed 'getting his hands dirty', so it was Oriana who had stolen into her father's chamber and suffocated him in his sleep. The only ones who know of the plot were Benway and Oriana. Not even Bricriu had been privy to that plan - better that he be kept in the dark along with

Eghan, in case the two-faced weasel decided to tell someone else in the settlement. He had his suspicions, no doubt, but that's all they were; and as long as Benway kept him involved in running the settlement, he doubted he'd have much trouble with him.

Oriana was quite a different matter, however, and he'd already begun to plot how he would dispose of her when the time came. It would need to be quick, that was certain, as she had a naturally suspicious nature and would, no doubt, notice any sudden changes in Benway's behaviour or routine. Until that time, however, she provided a pleasant enough diversion from the tedium of life in world without books, films, recreational drugs, the internet, soap (for Benway had failed to take into account just how pungent the aroma of human beings who rarely washed and wore the same clothes most of the time, could be) or even decent coffee - at least he had had the presence of mind to bring a good supply of instant with him otherwise he wouldn't have lasted a week.

Malvyn had encouraged their union at first - like many rulers, he was quite willing to pimp his daughter, in order to help his business relations. Oriana was not a woman who was content to be her father's bargaining chip, however. She had always known what was in her best interests and her betrothal to Henwas' son Ferghus was quickly forgotten. Whatever disapproval there might have been in the settlement (mostly raised by Ferghus himself) was also quashed when he suddenly disappeared a week or so later. Perhaps Malvyn should have noted then how quickly and dangerously his daughter's affections could change; but like many parents he failed to see her character flaws, even as she became more and more attached to Benway and the power he wielded.

It was now almost three months (though the time had passed so slowly that it had felt like double that amount), since Malvyn's death and Benway's ascension to ruler of the settlement. Since that time, he had been unable to leave for fear that his absence would trigger the revolt that, he knew, lay simmering just under the surface.

By conscripting the help of the outliers, Benway had managed to increase the productivity of the mine by 200%. Running shifts all day and all night, he would soon have gathered more than enough lepidolite to secure his position as the world leader in lithium production, then he could leave and get back to his own time - the real beauty being that as far as anyone else was concerned he had never left, because he and his men would return to the exact same moment. In the meantime, the lepidolite was stored in three large wagons, carefully guarded, ready for the day he decided it was time to leave.

Initially, he'd wanted to send the shipments back one-by-one, but he didn't want to run the risk that one or more of them might go missing or that his guards might decide to tell someone about either the portals or what he was up to. They were all well paid and had signed strict NDAs, but he knew that this wasn't foolproof. Mercenaries with the moral flexibility to oppress the enemies of whomever was paying them enough, would have little qualms about ripping off an untraceable shipment of lepidolite; so he'd kept both the men and lepidolite close at hand.

His 40th birthday was due at the end of the year and Benway knew that many of his critics were expecting him to fall headlong into some form of mid-life crisis. Little did they know he'd had what he felt to be some version of it here in the past. After all, what better way to stave off the feelings of inadequacy that many men feel when they reach the halfway point of their lives, than to become a virtual king, with the power of life and death over a tribe of primitive people. Like so many tyrants before him, Benway had found it easier to dehumanise the people of Aife's settlement - he found he could sleep better that way.

The arrival of Matthew Francis and this woman, Aife, had brought him back to reality though. He'd been expecting Matthew to turn up ever since he arrived. He knew he was after the lepidolite as well - that's why he'd come back to this time - however, it had taken so long for the two of them to cross paths that, in the end, Benway had almost forgotten about his rival until he'd been standing in front of him that afternoon. His arrival and subsequent removal, had been the last of the potential obstacles that Benway had expected to face and he realised that he could, at last, begin counting down the days until his work here was done.

Then he heard the screams and smelt the smoke.

[5]

By the time Anghus, Ethne and Idelisa reached the mine, Henwas and the others from the settlement had already killed the few guards surrounding the mine and freed those working there. The combined force then marched up the hill to the settlement.

Those on guard outside the broch were killed by plasma blasts from out of the darkness before they could return fire but their screams had alerted the guards near the community buildings and on the other side of the walkway and soon Anghus and the others were involved in a firefight whilst trying to get to the community buildings and free the outlier families trapped there. Stray plasma blasts soon set the both the broch and the community buildings alight. There were fires everywhere. Chaos ensued as the outliers and their families attempted to escape the flames only to face fire from the guards as they tried to get off the walkway.

"Turn back! Head for the other end of the walkway!" Anghus, who was near the edge of the walkway, shouted at them. Then he saw more guards approaching from that direction. He ran towards the community buildings firing at the nearest guards as he did so, whilst trying to dodge any blasts from the guards coming from the other end, but one blast clipped him in the side and he stumbled onto the wooden walkway. He still had the weapon in his hand, however, and managed to kill the last of the guards nearest to the buildings. "Go!" he shouted to the outliers who were clustered around him, "Take your families and get clear of the walkway, I'll hold the rest of the guards off as best I can."

They did not need to be told twice and headed quickly for the side of the walkway nearest the broch, whilst Anghus fired at the guards coming from the other end. He took out two of them before a blast hit him near the shoulder and he fell backwards.

"Anghus!" Idelisa screamed as she saw him fall. She wanted to run to him but Ethne held her back. She could see Anghus holding out his hand towards them, gesturing them to stay away. He looked across at them from where he lay, as the guards got closer, put his bloodied hand to his lips and blew Idelisa a kiss. Then, picking up his fallen weapon, he aimed it at the floor of the walkway just in front of the community buildings and fired. The floor exploded and the entire central section lurched violently down, pulling the buildings, the remaining guards and Anghus into the water and over the waterfall.

Idelisa collapsed sobbing into Ethne's arms and the two women sat there, huddled together, whilst the fighting continued around them. Anghus' sacrifice meant that the fight was now concentrated around the entrance to the broch. Many of the outliers picked up fallen weapons and joined the clash. Despite their defensive position inside the broch's entrance, Benway's guards were soon overrun and the outliers and the members of the settlement stormed into the broch looking for Benway and any remaining guards.

They found Bricriu hiding in a corner of the central chamber and dragged him, Benway and the last few guards to the edge of the waterfall. They threw the guards over the waterfall first and once he realised that the same thing would soon happen to him, Bricriu broke down and begged for his life. Unimpressed by his pleas for mercy, Henwas lifted him up on his shoulder and threw the pleading man over the edge of the waterfall all by himself. Benway himself said nothing at all. He no longer had his translator mask and anyway he knew it would be useless to try. His last thought as his body plummeted down towards the jagged rocks at the base of the waterfall was to wonder how everything could have gone wrong so quickly.

[6]

Aife and Morfran could already see smoke and a fiery glow coming from the small wood from some distance away and quickened their pace accordingly. When they reached the wood they found it ablaze and the smoke made it difficult to see anything at first. Then Aife heard Fionn whining and followed the sound until she discovered the wolf lying, wounded, next to Medb.

"Over here!" she shouted to Morfran, who came running over to her.

"I found two bodies, men dressed in white and the remains of the two black shapes but no sign...oh no!" He knelt down beside Medb and cradled her in his arms. Aife felt sure Medb must be dead, but at that moment she opened her eyes.

"Matthew," she said, as she looked up at his face, "I'm so sorry...this is all my fault."

"No it isn't, how could it be?" he replied, "what happened here?"

"Kynthelig...a trap..."

"How did he know to come here?"

"Me..." Her voice was weak and raspy. "He told me he'd spare Annan's life, if I took him and the others to where you'd be..."

"The others must be the two men you found," Aife suggested.

Morfran nodded. "What about Annan?" he asked Medb, "is he ok?"

"Escaped..." Medb managed to say with some difficulty. "Portal...Fionn and I tried to give him some time to get away, but Kynthelig went after him." Medb's breathing became shallower and then stopped altogether. Fionn whined pitifully. Aife stroked the wolf's ears. She could see several deep gashes on Fionn's side that were bleeding profusely.

Morfran pulled apart the bracelet on his wrist which contained the device that he'd used to contact Annan earlier, and handed it to Aife. He touched the screen and a series of numbers appeared.

"This is the moment in time that I met your father. Make sure Annan gives the co-ordinates of the mine to my younger self - but be careful! Remember, that moment effects everything that comes after it. Any changes you make will alter all our lives, even your father's. Now, go."

"Aren't you coming with me?"

"No," he said with a grimace, pointing at his own wound and then stroking Fionn's fur. "None of us can be of much help to you, now. You need to go on without us. Help Annan. Save us all."

Feeling the tears welling up inside her, Aife simply nodded and took the bracelet. As she headed off in the direction of the portal, only Fionn noticed somebody else following Aife through the smoke towards the archway, but she was too weak from her injuries to do anything other than whine pitifully once again.

chapter twelve:
the Right place at the
Right time

a s she neared the archway, Aife heard a faint sound behind her. She already knew who it was before the voice called out from behind her.

"Don't take another step."

Aife wondered whether she might have a chance of reaching the portal if she threw herself headfirst towards the archway. I could make it, she thought, it's only a few steps away. Knowing that whatever she did next would decide not only her fate, but that of Morfran, Medb, Fionn, and Annan as well, she decided not to. Instead she turned to face Oriana. She had picked up a fallen plasma weapon that had belonged to one of Kynthelig's companions.

"What will you do now, Oriana? Kill me?"

"I should do, but then what? Anghus and the others have no doubt taken back the settlement by now. If I go back, they'll kill me...so you'll take me with you."

"What if I say 'no'?"

"Then I'll kill your friends one by one," Oriana replied. Aife could tell that she meant it.

"Very well, I'll take you. You'll need the pendant that hangs around that man's neck," Aife said, pointing to body of the man in white, whose weapon Oriana held. "Without it you won't be able to pass through to the portal."

Keeping her weapon trained on Aife, Oriana knelt down beside the dead man and removed his pendant. "Lead on," she said to Aife, gesturing towards the archway.

In the sudden darkness of the portal Oriana grabbed ahold of Aife's arm, only releasing her grip once the various dials and knobs began to illuminate; then she moved over to the control panel with a gasp of wonder.

"It's so beautiful," she said, "like crystals glittering in the firelight. Do you understand everything that it does?"

"Yes. My friends from the future explained it to me. The most important control is this large wheel here, it controls whether you go forward or backwards in time. So, which direction do you want to go?"

"Forwards!" Oriana replied enthusiastically. "Benway told me a little about his time, I want to see it for myself."

"Very well..." Aife replied and turned the dial to the right so that the years spun past frighteningly fast whilst Oriana watched, mesmerised.

Seeing she was getting close, Aife released her grip on the wheel slightly and adjusted it in smaller increments, hoping she'd remembered the date correctly.

"Here we are," she said at last and subtly pushed the button for Zone 4 in such a way that she hoped Oriana barely noticed, "Benway's time, thousands of generations from our own."

"Good. Why don't you lead the way and show me," Oriana replied.

"As you wish..."

As soon as they were outside the portal they found themselves ankle deep in water.

"Why is the ground so wet?" Oriana asked angrily.

"We've come out into an indoor pool," Aife lied. "The people of this time have them to clean themselves regularly. Come on, it's this way." Aife began to climb the steps leading up from the basement and Oriana followed. When she neared the top Aife held her breath and then took the last step out into the barren wasteland. As soon as Oriana reached the top step she began to choke.

That was the moment Aife had been waiting for.

Spinning around, she punched Oriana in the face and sent her toppling backwards down the steps where she hit the water with a loud splash. Struggling for breath herself now, she raced back down the stairs to where Oriana was splashing about trying to find the weapon she'd dropped. Aife aimed a kick at Oriana's head and sent her reeling back into the shallow water.

That was when Aife became aware that they were not alone down there. Several figures were beginning to move towards them from out of the shadows.

"Welcome to the future, Oriana!" Aife said, as she ripped the pendant from her neck. "I hope you enjoy it!"

"No!" Oriana cried and tried to grab ahold of Aife's leg, but Aife kicked her away once more and ran towards the portal. She heard Oriana begin to scream as the basement dwellers got hold of her, then the sound was abruptly cut off as she entered the blackness of the portal.

(2)

Unlike Aife, Annan didn't have the exact co-ordinates of the moment in time when Morfran had first met Aife's father and had to trust his memory of what the numbers on the control panel had been when his father had taken Aife and him there. As such, he arrived about five minutes earlier than he was supposed to. Guessing at once what he'd done he turned the situation to his advantage.

"Father!" he called out the trees around him. "If you're here, I need your help!"

[3]

After dealing with Medb and the wolf, Kynthelig made his way to the portal. He silently cursed himself for not bringing more men with him. The battle had been a near thing and in the end Annan had managed to escape with the compass. However, Kynthelig knew the portals better than anyone - he'd help build them. Because of this, he knew something that Morfran and the others did not. How to make the portal recall the previous moment in time it had been to. He smiled as the date and time that Annan had travelled to appeared on a screen on the control panel and set the controls of the portal so that he could arrive two minutes earlier.

[4]

"There's no one here, lad," said Kynthelig in reply to Annan's call for help. He stepped out from behind one of the trees, with his weapon drawn. "Your father's younger self won't arrive for another five minutes. You've no more options left. Drop your weapon and give me the compass or I'll kill both of you."

Annan let his weapon fall to the floor. "Do you know what your greatest weakness is?" You keep underestimating me and my father. Especially my father. If you'd really been paying attention you'd have know that he'd never give up trying to save the world, as long there was still breath left in him. You'd also know how important this moment that we're in right now was to him...that's why he travelled here more than once!"

Annan threw himself to the ground as the wood erupted in volley of plasma fire as various Morfrans from the past came out of the trees on both sides and opened fire on Kynthelig, who was forced to run for cover.

[5]

Back in the portal, Aife spun the large dial to the left until the numbers on the control panel matched those Morfran had given her. She dashed out of the portal and into a battlefield.

For a second she thought she'd gotten the numbers wrong, that she was in some other moment in time. Then she saw Annan running towards her.

"Get down, take cover!" Annan shouted at her. Kynthelig saw his chance and felled Annan with single plasma blast to the back. The compass fell from his hand and tumbled to the ground in front of Aife.

"No!" she screamed. She picked up the compass and ran to him. As she cradled him in her arms, he smiled up at her.

"You got away," he said, "what about my father?"

Aife shook her head. "He was hurt. He wanted to stay with Medb and Fionn. He told me to go and help you, but I'm too late..."

With the last bit of strength left in him, he pulled her close and kissed her. "I'm glad you're here...and there's no such thing as 'too late', look..."

Aife followed his gaze and saw the earlier version of herself, Annan and Morfran emerge from the archway. She looked back at Annan but it was too late, he was dead. Wiping a tear from her eye, she threw the compass towards the trio by the portal. "Make sure Matthew gets this..." she said and just had time to kiss Annan's now lifeless lips before a blast from Kynthelig killed her as well. Reacting quicker than the other two, Morfran grabbed the compass from the ground and managed to push both Aife and Annan back through the archway before more plasma blasts raked the ground where they had been standing.

"I don't understand...what just happened?" Aife asked, once they were back inside the portal.

"The past has changed, our future selves came here to give the co-ordinates of the mine to my younger self and someone is trying to stop that happening," Morfran replied as he frantically readjusted the controls. "My younger self will arrive at the moment in time in a few moments. If he is killed, then everything we're trying to do will be for nothing. I will be dead, Annan will never have been born, and if I'm prevented from meeting your father then the chances are, you would not be here either."

"Ok, so we go back to the moment just before he goes through the portal and give him the compass," Annan suggested.

"It's more complicated than that, I'm afraid," said Morfran. "If he never comes through the portal, then none of the events that happened afterwards would take place. That includes our future selves finding the co-ordinates of the mine and recording them into the compass. Not only will we disappear from this moment, but so does the compass."

"So how do we give you, the younger you, the co-ordinates?" Aife asked.

"I have an idea," Morfran replied, "I just hope it works."

(6)

After a shower and a late breakfast, Matthew made his way to the basement of the apartment block. His bag was packed, he'd checked everything at least twice, his search for the mine could finally begin. When got out of the lift in the basement he found Morfran and a young man and young woman, about his age, dressed in bronze age clothes, waiting for him.

"Morfan? What are you doing here?"

"As ironic as it sounds, Matthew, there's no time to explain. Take out the compass that I asked you to get." Matthew did as he was told and tried to hand his compass over to Morfran but the older man pushed it away. "No," he said. "You need to do it." He held up his own compass, pressed a button on the display and some numbers came up. "These are the co-ordinates of the mine, copy them into your device, do it quickly and make sure you don't make any mistakes."

"But I don't understand...why did you tell me to get hold of a compass if you already had the co-ordinates?" Matthew asked as he copied the numbers from Morfran's compass into his.

"I didn't. That was another version of me, of you in fact, because I am you - an older version of you that soon won't exist anymore just like the version of me that told you to find a compass of your own. This is your son, Adam..." he said indicating Annan, "and this Aife, the daughter of the man you would have encountered when you went through the portal into the past." Matthew looked at the two of them and that saw they they were holding hands. "Now that moment has been changed by someone from the future wanting to stop you finding the mine and saving the world," Morfran continued, "if you go there now, you will be killed and all this will be for nothing. That's why we came to give you the co-ordinates. When you no longer go through the portal to that moment everything will change, however, and we and our compass, which future versions of ourselves gave their lives to obtain, will no longer exist - that's why you needed to enter the co-ordinates into your device."

"So, you're telling me if I find the mine in my time, then the plan will work? The world will be saved?"

"The attempts of those from the future to stop us getting the co-ordinates of the mine, would suggest that, yes...but if I were you, I'd make doubly sure and begin the change that bit earlier."

"When?"

"You'll figure it out, I'm sure. Take care of yourself in the future..."

"...and in the past." Matthew replied to the empty basement. The other three had disappeared.

chapter thirteen: everything changes again

(1)

All of a sudden the shooting stopped. Kynthelig came out from behind the tree where he'd been sheltering and found the small wood suddenly deserted and the bodies of Annan and Aife were no longer lying there. He realised what had happened. Morfran must have warned his younger self not to travel back here. There was no use waiting here any longer. As he made his way back to the portal he saw Medb, standing in front the archway, looking at him.

"It seems as if I'm no longer needed here," she said with a wry smile on her lips.

"Get out of my way, unless you want me to kill you a second time today."

"Maybe you should just except the fact that you've failed..." Medb said, as she moved aside.

"Not while there's still breath left in my body."

"Be careful what you wish for..." she said to herself, once he'd passed into the portal.

[2]

Llyr had been setting up his camp for the night when he heard some loud bangs and the occasional bright flash of light coming from the small wood on the hill above him. At first he thought it was thunder breaking over head. The midsummer air had felt the way it always did when a storm was due that day, but when he realised that the noise seemed to be coming from within the wood itself, he picked up his bow and went to investigate.

When he reached the wood, the acrid stench of smoke still hung there in the evening air. Several of the trees looked like they had scorch marks on them, but no one was there. He wandered a short way into the wood and looked around some more but could find nothing except a few more scorch marks on the ground and the stone archway that stood there in the middle of the clearing.

He put his hand to it and felt the cold stone under his fingertips. Something inside then compelled him to touch the pendant featuring the lump of the crystal mined in his settlement, that his father had given him on the start of his journey into the hills, to see what settlements might be found to trade with there. The trip had been fruitful, he'd found a number of settlements that had expressed an interest in trading for their crystal and tomorrow he would begin the journey back home again.

Reassured that there was nothing that he needed to concern himself with in the wood, he went back down to his camp, cooked the rabbit he had caught earlier that day and by the time he eventually fell asleep under the starry sky, he had all but forgotten about the noises and lights in the wood.

[3]

Using the same technique as before, Kynthelig was able to retrieve the last set of co-ordinates in time the portal had travelled to and then adjust them to arrive in the basement of Matthew's apartment block five minutes earlier.

He smiled to himself as he exited the portal and stood directly in front of the door to the utility rooms, ready to blast Morfran and the others as soon as they came through. He barely heard the ping of the lift arriving and only turned when the doors opened directly behind him and Matthew swung the heavy golf club that hit him square in the forehead and knocked him to the ground.

By the time Morfran and the others arrived in the basement a few minutes later, the only sign of either Matthew or Kynthelig having been there were a few spots of blood on the floor by the lift doors, which nobody noticed.

When Kynthelig finally came to he found himself tied to the base of a tree in the middle of a wood. Matthew stood in front of him still holding the golf club.

"You're coming 'round...that's good. I'd hate to have to just leave you here, without any explanation."

"Why didn't you just kill me?" Kynthelig asked as he struggled against the rope that bound him.

"Because firstly, I'm not a killer. Secondly because whatever I do to you it won't matter once I've accomplished what I need to do on my next trip. This moment will cease to exist and hopefully you with it. I just needed to make sure you didn't alter the moment when my older self gave me the co-ordinates of the mine. That's why I went back 10 minutes to make sure you weren't lying in wait for them, just as they told me you'd done before. It's also why I'm taking this..." he held up Kynthelig's spiral pendant "...and leaving you here. This is as far back as the portal would let me take you - year one as far as it's concerned. I have no idea what, if any, form of human settlers there are around here at the moment, so I'll take your key just to be on the safe side. As you seem to care so much about the existence of the portals, I felt it was only fitting you could be here for their beginning, as well as their end."

With that, Matthew walked back to the archway, ignoring Kynthelig's shouts and curses until, by passing into the portal once more, they were blocked out entirely.

[5]

The house was dark that evening when Matthew's father returned. His wife was staying with her parents for a few days and with no one to hurry home to, he'd been out celebrating the success of the dig with his young team of archeologists and was now convinced that he'd probably had at least one drink too many. As he fumbled, slightly woozily, for the light switch in the study, a voice spoke to him from out of the darkness.

"You've had cause to celebrate."

Finally finding the light switch, Matthew's father turned on the small table lamp and saw a young man of about 15, with blond hair, sitting in one of the armchairs, near the fireplace.

"Do I know you?" he asked the young man.

"Not really, not yet anyhow."

"If you've broken in here looking for things to steal, then I'm afraid you've made a mistake. Aside from the small amount of money I have on my person, which I will happily give you if you promise to leave. There's nothing of any real value in this house."

"I'm not here to take anything," the young man replied, "quite the opposite. I'm here to give something."

"What might that be?"

"Something that will change the course of your life. Maybe you should have a seat first though, you look as if you might fall over any minute."

"I'm fine..."

"Please come and sit down anyway, what I have to tell you is very important - it concerns the material you've recently unearthed during your latest dig."

Wary and still slightly drunk, Matthew's father made his way over to the armchair directly opposite the young man and sat down. "What do you know about my dig?" he asked.

"I know you found some unusual things: a sword with a symbol like one third of a triskelion at its hilt, that looks like it's made of bronze, but it's not. When you eventually have it analysed you'll discover it's been forged using a metal created from elements not found on this planet. You also found a lepidolite crystal."

"How do you know all this? We only completed the dig this afternoon, we're still cataloguing the finds..."

"How I know isn't important," the young man interrupted, "what's important is that you take what I'm about to tell you, seriously. If you need further proof of how much I know, then let me offer you my congratulations on becoming a father. Your wife informed you that she's pregnant two days ago. The child will be a boy. You will name him Matthew, after your maternal grandfather."

Matthew's father looked pale. "Why are you telling me all this?" he asked.

"Because the lepidolite is more important than you know. It came from a mine nearby, one that has been forgotten for thousands of years. It is the biggest natural supply of it in these parts and I need you to find it again and mine it for lithium"

"But I don't know anything about mining lithium - I'm an archeologist..."

"Not anymore. From now on, you need to be in lithium mining business. Your future, your son's future and even your grandson's future, depends on you doing this, not to mention millions of other people all over the world. Someone once told me that to change the world quickly, you need both a commodity that people want and a level of influence. You come from a wealthy family, money and resources are not a problem for you. Once you have claimed the land containing the lepidolite mine, you will have the commodity, but all of this is simply a means to an end. You need to use it to help pull humanity back from the brink of extinction by slowing climate change. Use the money and the influence the lithium production will give you to literally save the world and, in turn, support clean energy and keep lithium production out of the hands of conglomerates that want to keep that resource for themselves. On no account are you to sell shares in the mine or the lithium to anyone who simply wants to profit from it. That way you can be sure that what you're doing will help the planet and by setting these conditions you also insure that anyone who wants to use the lithium you produce is working towards the same goal."

"It sounds amazing and, of course, I care about what happens to the planet but...the scale of the undertaking you're describing, it could take..."

"Lifetimes. Yes. What I've described will be your life's work. Your unborn son's too. That's why it has to start with you, that's why I'm asking you to change the course of your life and take up this burden. It will be hard for you, at least at first, but you have an army of business managers and lawyers who can help you and as your power and influence grows, so will your retinue. Eventually you will have more than enough people to support your work and your example will encourage others to take up the cause, but it all starts with you. You should know that if you do this, you will succeed - I can promise you that. Hopefully this knowledge will help keep you going at the beginning. More importantly, you will end your life knowing you have done the one thing most people can only dream of doing: you will have changed the world for the better."

"Supposing I believe you and say that I'll do it. How do I start?"

The young man leaned over to him and held out a piece of paper. "These are the G.P.S. co-ordinates of the mine. Write them down. Everything else will follow on from there."

Matthew's father took the proffered piece of paper and copied the numbers written on it onto a notepad. When he looked up again the young man had disappeared. Then he realised that the piece of paper the young man had given him was gone too.

All that was left were the numbers he'd written down.

(6)

Matthew's father was as good as his word. Within a week of his visit from the strange young man, he'd bought the land where the mine stood and begun the process of uncovering it after thousands of years.

By the time Matthew was born, the mine was operational.

By the time of Matthew's fifth birthday, his father had become the largest supplier of lithium in that part of the world and had helped to successfully lobby for a worldwide ban on the use of fossil fuels.

Shortly after Matthew's fifteenth birthday, his father died suddenly and Matthew took control of the business. In amongst his father's papers, Matthew found a letter addressed to him from his father.

Dear Son,

I hope I will have the opportunity one day to talk to you about all this in person, as it seems wrong to try and do it through a letter. However, after some recent health issues I felt it was important to put all this down in writing, just in case. I know better than most how quickly our futures can change.

As you are well aware, I've given over most of my life to producing lithium from lepidolite extracted from a mine near here. When I die, this running of this business will pass to you. You'll probably have a lot of people giving you advice when that happens, some might even suggest selling some shares in the mine or some of the lithium that we produce to our competitors in exchange for a quick profit but implore you not to do this and I feel it is only fair to explain why.

I didn't discover the location of the mine by accident. Some months before you were born, I was visited by a young man who told me its exact location. As well as telling me where to find the mine, he also insisted that both the lithium and the profits must only be used to support clean energy products and initiatives and to use the political influence that the mine would inevitably bring to exert pressure on the government and the various energy concerns in order to prevent catastrophic climate change.

I know how ridiculous that all sounds. I never told anyone else about the young man's visit, not even your mother, for fear that they'd think I'd completely lost my mind. However, everything that the young man said turned out to be true, including various pieces of information that it is hard to know how he could have come by through any rational explanation, so I have tried *my best of to do what he asked of me and I hope that, in doing so, I have managed to make some small difference.*

On my death, this task will be passed on to you and I hope that you too will do your best to see it through. I am sorry, if it comes to that, to have leave you with a task and even a career that you haven't chosen for yourself. I know full well, what it's like to have expectations placed on you by your parents. I had hoped that perhaps I would be able to change things enough in my lifetime that you would be spared having to devote your life to it as well, but change (real change, that is) can often take far longer than we expect. If this proves to be the case, I hope at least that you'll see that it was worth doing.

Whatever happens, please know that I am immensely proud of you and the man you are becoming and always will be.

Dad

Matthew closed the letter and put it in his wallet. There would be many occasions over the coming months and years when he would re-read the letter, often after a particularly trying meeting with his various business managers and lawyers. When he did so he would smile to himself, knowing that in the end he would be proved right.

In the wake of his father's death, some of the finds from the various archaeological digs he'd participated in were bequeathed to various museums. However, one item listed was unable to be located anywhere amongst the collection.

It was a bronze sword with a spiral emblem at the hilt.

In her fifteenth year, Llyr encouraged Aife to travel and see if she might be able to find new settlements, farther down the river, open to trade for the crystal that they mined. It was an idea that the council were also in favour of, particularly Malvyn, who suggested that his own daughter, Oriana, also accompany Aife, along with Aife's cousin Cahal.

The three of them were due to begin their journey that morning so, determined to enjoy the last bit of time she'd have to herself for a while, Aife had risen before dawn and headed down the slope to the water's edge.

As she sat there, watching the first pinky bronze rays of the sun, break over the trees on the far hills to her left, she thought about the upcoming trip downriver. She was happy that Oriana, who had been one of her best friends since childhood, was coming with her. The two of them had bonded together as daughters of council members who both strained a little against the roles prescribed to them. There was talk that the council might relax their rule against female descendants taking over their father's position on the council. There was even talk about them abolishing hereditary succession to the council all together and allowing the community to vote on whomever should replace a member once they died.

Truth be told, Aife wasn't interested either way.

She'd seen how her friend Ethne had dealt with life on her own after her father's death, two springs previously, and knew that she could happily live with her if she were no longer able to live in the broch. She already sensed, that unlike her good friends Idelisa and Anghus or even Oriana and Cahal (whose romance seemed to blossom with each passing day), she didn't need to be with anyone in order to be happy. What she wanted more than anything, was to have her own life and make her own decisions. She had no idea how far the three of them might travel, perhaps to the very end of the river, but she had already begun she think about not returning with them.

At that moment, through the trees on the other side of the river, Aife caught a glimpse of something white moving there. Then, suddenly, at a place where there was a gap in forest, she saw it.

A wolf, completely white, except for some grey on its tail and forepaws.

It stood completely still and looked across the river at Aife. She could see no sign of other members of its pack, so Aife guessed the wolf must be a lone one - a female, probably. She didn't want the wolf to bolt for cover if she saw her move, so Aife stayed completely still and just watched the creature.

The wolf did the same, as if the two of them shared some connection that neither wanted to break. Aife realised that she was holding her breath. Still not taking her eyes from Aife, the wolf moved down to the water's edge and drank thirstily. Then, with an almost imperceptible nod of her beautiful white head, the wolf moved back into the trees and was soon lost from view.

Aife got up from where she'd been sitting and made her way back up the slope towards her settlement, but her thoughts lingered on the wolf. It was a sign, she told herself. She, like the wolf, could and would manage just fine on her own. She began to think of her upcoming journey with new enthusiasm.

Everything would change from this point onwards.

acknowledgements

Book writing is always a lengthy process, but some books have a longer gestation than others. In this case, the idea was one I'd been carrying around in my head since I was about 12. I'd extemporised a version of it on a long walk with my father. He thought it showed real promise and encouraged me to write it down, but as the years went by the story seemed to slip further and further from my grasp. It would take my father's death in 2014, to suggest a way back into the story, which I would finally begin to write in 2018 after I'd completed *Solid State Memories,* This book is dedicated to his memory.

Any piece of creative work is inevitably some form of compromise between the ephemeral version that the artist imagines in their head and the finished piece. This book isn't and could never be the same as the idea that I imagined all those years ago, but I'd like to think that the 12 year old me would have approved of what I've now come up with.

This book is obviously a work of fiction and as such has a tenuous grip on historical accuracy at times. However, I did do a certain amount of reading about pre-Roman Britain prior to starting writing and am particularly indebted to Francis Pryor's superb *Britain*

251

B.C. which furnished me with a lot of useful detail about Bronze Age dwellings and lifestyle - even if I did subsequently mix elements from different periods and areas - and is well worth a read if you're interested in learning about the era.

Because of the extraordinary length of time it has taken for this book to finally make its way out into the world, I am extra grateful to my friends and readers who generously agreed to look through the manuscript and offer their feedback: Stephen Ball, Gavin Brick, Caroline Selkirk and Lee Thompson.

I would also like to thank Nick Langley and Mat Smith for their help and feedback in getting this book ready for publication.

I must also thank my wife, Heidi, and our two children, Benjamin and Rebecca, for their enormous patience over the course of the last 3 years whenever I would start talking about this book.

Above all, I'm pleased that a version of it now resides in these pages and not merely in my head. Now, it also belongs to you.

Rupert Lally
April 2022

Solid State Memories

What would you do if the person you loved most in the world was gone and no-one remembered them?

Dr Alex Wells wakes up to find her partner, Rachel, missing and her own nanotechnology implanted in her. Fleeing sinister government agents and unable to trust either her colleagues or her own memories, she must piece together what happened to her before it's too late.

In his debut novella, musician turned author Rupert Lally draws inspiration from the likes of J.G. Ballard and Philip K. Dick in a speculative sci-fi story about the nature of memory.

Printed in Great Britain
by Amazon

82597357R00154